MOST

Likely to

KILL

Totally
80s
Mysteries
Book 2

Books by D.A. Wilkerson

Totally 80s Mysteries

A Totally Killer Wedding
Most Likely to Kill
Of Heist and Men

Mystery Journals

Mysterious Musings
My Totally Suspect Notebook

MOST *Likely to* KILL

D.A. Wilkerson
Mystery Author
danawilkerson.com

Most Likely to Kill
Totally 80s Mysteries Book 2
by D.A. Wilkerson

© 2022 Dana Wilkerson

Designed in the USA
Images and fonts used under license by Canva

Published by Dana Wilkerson, LLC
Edmond, OK
danawilkerson.com

First Edition: July 2022

Paperback ISBN: 978-1-948148-32-0
eBook ISBN: 978-1-948148-33-7

Dedicated to the Class of 1975

CHERRY HILL HIGH SCHOOL CLASS OF 1975

Class Officers

President: Cheryl Young
Vice-President: Jeff Jenkins
Secretary: Beckett Monahan
Treasurer: Billy Arbuckle

Class Superlatives

Most Popular: Cheryl Young and Randy Stouffer
Most Athletic: Trixie McCoy and Jeff Jenkins
Most Likely to Succeed: Billy Arbuckle
Most Likely to Teach at CHHS: Donna Daly
Easiest to Embarrass: Beckett Monahan
Best Dressed: Paula Olean
Biggest Flirt: Kyle Korte
Noisiest: Karla James
Quietest: Anita Nichols

ONE

I DON'T KNOW WHO decided senior class officers should be in charge of high school reunions, but the idea was ridiculous. "Vote for me because I'll get a soda machine put in the cafeteria" does not necessarily later translate into "I'll do a fantastic job of organizing a party for seventy people scattered all over Missouri and beyond every five years for the rest of my life."

However, that's the way it works, so as the senior class secretary of the Cherry Hill High School class of 1975, I was automatically a member of the reunion committee until the end of time. That's not to say I can't plan big parties. I can organize any event you want to throw at me. The problem is having to do it with three people who couldn't plan their way out of a refrigerator box.

I did make one questionable decision while planning our upcoming ten-year reunion, though. The "Welcome Back Class of '75" banner strung up across Main Street in downtown Cherry Hill looked totally fabulous. The issue was its precise location. One end was attached to the apartment above The Checkered Cloth diner—otherwise known as "The Check"—while the other was tied to First Community Church's education and office annex.

The idea had seemed fine in the morning, as I told the city workers where to hang it. However, as I sat at my desk in the church office in the afternoon, I could hear the vinyl flapping in the breeze outside my window. The loud and inconsistent noise was distracting and starting to give me a headache. I stepped to the window and shook my fist at the banner, as if it wasn't all my own fault.

A few seconds later, the door to the inner office opened, and Pastor Harold Coker poked his head out. "Beckett, is that sound driving you up the wall, too?"

"Yes. Sorry."

"You don't need to be sorry. It's not your fault." He walked over and peered out the window.

"Actually, it is."

"Ah. Well, I can't focus with that racket, so I'm heading to the house. Call over if you need anything."

"Will do."

Unfortunately, I didn't have the luxury of going home, since I needed to stay and answer the phone. I also needed to finish typing up the church bulletin and make copies before signing off for the weekend.

Office hours at First Comm are from 8:30–5:00 on Mondays through Thursdays. We get Fridays off since we work Wednesday evenings and Sunday mornings. Even though I'm the secretary and not a pastor, I have responsibilities during service times, like ensuring the scheduled workers show up for nursery duty and taking care of choir robe emergencies. I also help our youth pastor, Greg Villanova, with the youth group on Wednesday evenings.

I double-checked the giant church calendar on the wall behind my desk to make sure I had typed all the correct dates in the bulletin for upcoming events, and I yanked the ditto master out of my typewriter so fast I nearly ripped it. I breathed a huge sigh of relief when I realized it was still intact and I crossed the office to start the old, clunky ditto machine.

While the machine made its rhythmic *kerplunk* sound across the room and the chemical smell of the fluid filled the small space, I sat at my desk and made a list of all the things I still needed to do to get ready for the reunion. That night I was going to Jazzercise, which meant I wouldn't be able to accomplish much else. Most of the rest of the tasks would have to wait until the next day or even Saturday morning.

While getting Fridays off work is a nice perk, practically everyone else works on Fridays, so nobody else on the reunion committee was free to spend much time helping prepare the 4-H Building at the fairgrounds for the big day on Saturday.

Some people might find it odd we were holding the reunion at the fairgrounds, but the newly renovated 4-H Building was the biggest, nicest venue in town. The fair board chose the structure as the one building on the site to insulate and equip with a full kitchen. They had even sprung for heating and air conditioning.

Brrrrring!

"Hello, First Community Church. This is Beckett."

"Hey Beck."

"What's up, Trix?"

"We still on for tomorrow?"

"Yep. Meet me at the fairgrounds at ten. Bring the kids if you want."

"They'll just slow us down. I'll drop them off with my mom."

"Okay. See you then."

My lifelong best friend Trixie didn't work in the summer, since she taught math at the high school, and I had been able to twist her arm into helping me with the reunion. She was neither a class officer nor a party planner, but she felt she owed me one for staying with her two kids overnight while she and Scott went away to celebrate their ninth anniversary a few weekends earlier. Plus, Trixie was in excellent physical shape and would be a big help when it came time to move tables and chairs.

I was nowhere near to being in excellent shape, though I was currently in the best shape of my life. When Trixie and I were nine, we were playing in a tree in her front yard when I fell out and broke my leg in three places. The bones weren't set right, so I have a permanent limp. I've used that as an excuse to not play sports or exercise for most of my life. But with the reunion looming, I decided it was finally time to act. Nothing motivates quite like the prospect of seeing dozens of your old friends and enemies all at once.

As a result, a couple months earlier I started going to Jazzercise with my aunt Starla, who is ten years my senior. Thanks to my bad leg, I am anything but graceful. But Jazzercise was fun, and I'd lost a few pounds and gained some energy.

When the copies were done, I sat at Greg's desk to fold them, since my desk was an absolute disaster. Greg was only a part-time church employee, so he didn't work on Thursdays, and I knew he wouldn't mind me using his area. Folding paper after paper in half was a mindless task, and my mind wandered to my secondary reason for Jazzercise: I had an actual date for the first time in more than two years!

This dry spell was not due to my couch-potato tendencies but because of my track record with men. I have this problem of falling for men who need "fixing." As someone who absolutely lives to help people, I have a history of being drawn to men with issues like an ant making a beeline to a picnic.

To break myself of this habit, I didn't accept any dates when I moved back to Cherry Hill after breaking things off with my fiancé Walter two years earlier. I didn't trust myself to choose wisely anymore, so I said no across the board to all men. It didn't take long for word to get around town that I wasn't in the market for a man, so they soon stopped asking. Though my mother never stopped asking me when I was going to find myself a nice man—or any man—and settle down.

A few months earlier, however, two men who were new to town had started showing interest in me. One was a bit unfortunate, as it was Greg. While he was cute and funny, I was not attracted to him in the least. He moved to Cherry Hill right before Christmas, and I was so far out of the dating game I didn't even realize he was interested in me until Trixie pointed it out after my birthday party in March. When he finally got up the nerve to ask me out on a date a few weeks later, I tactfully turned him down. Thankfully, he took it well, and we remained friends. But Trixie was convinced he still carried a torch for me.

The other man was a whole different story. I met Mitchell Crowe on the night of my birthday party when he tagged along with Aunt Star's boyfriend Darren. Darren Turley is the Deputy Police Chief in Cherry Hill, and the department had brought Mitchell in from Jefferson City to help solve a murder.

Thunk!

My head automatically turned toward the window, and my arm jerked. I caught the stack of folded bulletins before they slid onto the floor, and I crossed the room to peer out the window. Veronica Coker, the pastor's wife, stood on the sidewalk below the window tapping one foot impatiently. I slid the window up.

"It's about time," she said. "Let me in." She climbed the handful of steps to the door and gave me an expectant look.

I slammed the window shut, hurried out into the hall, and opened the outside door for her.

"Thanks." She strode down the hallway and said over her shoulder, "I got over here and realized I left my key at home."

Her home was all the way across the parking lot.

"Okay," I called after her. I would have said more, but she had already rounded the corner and was gone. I shrugged and went back into the office.

Cherry Hill isn't a town where doors are typically locked. But ever since the murder, I was a tad jumpy. I started locking the house and even my car sometimes, and when I was alone in the church, I also locked myself in. That made things a little inconvenient for visitors, but it made me feel safe.

I still found it difficult to believe someone was killed here in Cherry Hill. Our small town has a murder about once every forty years, which is why our police department needed Mitchell's assistance with the investigation. And not only was there a murder, but it happened at First Comm, and I discovered the body!

While I'm not usually one to toot my own horn, I'm also not too humble to admit that I was instrumental in catching the killer. Strangely enough, Veronica had helped me solve the crime.

Unfortunately, the circumstances that brought Mitchell to Cherry Hill also prevented us from acting on the sparks that flew between us from the moment we first locked eyes. Since he was an investigating officer and I was a witness, we couldn't start any kind of romantic relationship without potentially compromising the murder investigation. We could have been stuck in that limbo for years, but luckily the murderer confessed and pleaded guilty, so I wasn't required to appear in court, and the case was resolved quickly.

As soon as Mitchell filed the final case paperwork, he called me, we talked for hours, and he asked me out on a date for the following weekend. And what happened? Before the day arrived, Mitchell was sent to *another* town in a far-flung corner of the state to help investigate a bank robbery.

We had talked on the phone several times when he had a few minutes to spare, and he had readily agreed to be my reunion date if his schedule would allow. He was supposed to wrap up his current assignment and be back in Jeff City sometime this week, though it hadn't happened yet. My chest constricted at even the thought he might be delayed.

The office door suddenly opened, and my arm jerked again. This time I sent half the bulletins spinning out onto the floor. Greg apologized, dropped to the ground, and swept them up into a pile before I could even attempt to get to my feet.

"Sorry! I was in my own little world, and you startled me." I checked my watch. "Goodness, I didn't realize it's almost 5:00 already."

Greg tapped the stack of papers against the desktop to straighten them. "No need to apologize," he said in his Southern drawl. "I stopped by to grab a couple books."

I started to stand, but Greg waved me back down. He pulled up a chair on the other side of his desk and started folding bulletins.

"Your class reunion is this weekend."

"Yes." I wondered where he was going with that statement, as he knew all about it. I had talked about the reunion planning so much that Veronica banned me from even mentioning it in her presence. There was also no way Greg had missed the banner over the street.

He looked down. "Do you ... um, I mean, are you taking anyone with you?"

"I am."

His eyes shot to mine. I hadn't mentioned anything about Mitchell to anyone but Trixie and Aunt Star, so his surprise was not unwarranted.

"Mitchell Crowe is going with me."

Greg raised his eyebrows. "Mitchell? The cop from your birthday?"

"The detective, yes."

He pressed his lips together tightly for a moment before saying, "I see."

Did he, though? Perhaps Trixie was right, and he wasn't fully fine with us just being friends. Had he hoped I'd say I didn't have a date and would ask him out of desperation? If so, there was nothing I could do about that.

"It should be fun!" I patted the stack of bulletins. "There. All done. Thanks for your help." This time when I stood, he didn't try to stop me.

———

THE PHONE WAS RINGING when I walked into the house. I rushed across the kitchen to answer it before the other person gave up.

"Hello?" I panted from the exertion.

"Beckett, are you okay?"

I smiled at the sound of the voice on the line. "Mitchell! Yes, I'm fine. I ran into the house to catch the phone. How are you? *Where* are you?"

"Well, I hate to tell you this ..." he trailed off.

A lump formed in my throat.

"... but I'm back home!"

If I could have reached him, I would have playfully smacked him. Scratch that. If I could have reached him, I would have done something much more pleasant.

He said he'd be spending the next day and Saturday morning at the police station in Jeff City, but he would leave work in time to make it to Cherry Hill before the reunion started at 3:00.

I was tempted to skip Jazzercise and keep talking to him, but Aunt Star would be home soon, and she would drag me out the door with her regardless of what I was doing or wearing. Since I didn't want to go to Jazzercise in my pencil skirt, button-up blouse, pantyhose, and flats, I wrapped up the call.

My entire body was tingling as I climbed the stairs to my room. I really hoped Mitchell didn't have any major issues I'd need to deal with or, more importantly, try to fix. Aunt Star had asked Darren to find out, but he flat-out refused to get involved.

A door slammed downstairs, followed by quick footsteps on the stairs. Aunt Star appeared in my doorway as I was trying to decide between my hot pink or purple leggings. She picked up the pink ones and thrust them into my chest.

"Wear the pink. Be ready in five minutes." She left as quickly as she had arrived. Her bedroom door closed, and a few seconds later the sounds of Tears for Fears faintly reached my ears.

"Turn it up!" I hollered.

The volume increased.

"Thanks!"

I struggled into my spandex pants, slipped on an oversized purple T-shirt, tied up my Reeboks, and corralled my naturally curly auburn hair into a turquoise scrunchie. I yelled to Aunt Star that I was ready and headed downstairs.

While I waited, I sat at the glass-topped kitchen table and twirled a napkin ring around my finger. I had personally never owned a napkin ring, but this was Aunt Star's house, and she was much fancier than me. Sometimes I wished I lived alone, but I was extremely grateful my aunt let me live with her rent free, though I did pitch in for half of the phone, cable TV, and utilities.

I could never afford to live somewhere as nice as Aunt Star's house on my church secretary salary. Plus, I was also making a car payment, since my old car was destroyed by the murderer back in March. The insurance check for my beige, hand-me-down, four-door 1968 Ford Torino was understandably small. So now I was making monthly payments on my new-old 1980 bright yellow Ford Pinto.

The new car was much more my style, but sometimes I missed the old one. It had been Grandma Pearl's car before she gave it to me for my high school graduation. I had made a lot of memories in that old Torino—a few I'd rather forget, but the vast majority made me smile.

Aunt Star pounded down the stairs and struck a pose in front of me in her spandex outfit. She looked like Princess Di from the neck up and Jane Fonda from the neck down. She was even wearing leg warmers, though it was pushing 100 degrees outside.

She waved me toward the door. "Let's go."

I followed her out and buckled myself into her almost-brand-new candy-apple-red Camaro Z28. Like I said, Aunt Star is fancy. She had been the top-selling Realtor in Cherry County every year for the past 10 years. As the owner and broker of Hilltop Realty, she could sit back and make money by letting her agents do all the buying and selling, but that had never been her style.

As we rode through town, she cranked up the radio to get us in the mood. We sang along to "Walking on Sunshine" as we cruised through town.

We pulled into a parking spot next to a car I didn't recognize, and the driver stepped out in full workout gear. She slammed the door and took a quick glance down through my window as she started toward the studio door. A few seconds later she stopped, turned, and gave me a piercing look.

TWO

I TENTATIVELY WAVED TO Karla James Bright. My former classmate whipped her long, black hair behind her shoulders, put her hands on her hips, and stared at me until I stepped out of the car. Aunt Star's slamming door moved Karla's attention to the other side of the vehicle, but her expression didn't change.

Aunt Star put her own hands on her hips. "Karla James, what's your problem?"

"It's Karla Bright. And my problem is that the two of you," she pointed at each of us in turn, "thought my brother was a murderer."

Karla made an excellent point. Aunt Star and I had, indeed, briefly wondered if her brother Marty had killed Aidan Patrick a few months ago. He had not. Marty quickly forgave us, much to his credit, but apparently Karla was holding a grudge.

"You know what?" Aunt Star said. "That was a very stressful time, the killer was coming after Beckett, and we were on a focused mission to follow up every clue before my niece here," she jabbed her finger in my direction, "ended up in Cherry Hill Cemetery. We apologized to your brother, and he understood. I think you should try to do the same."

Karla huffed, crossed her arms, and looked back and forth between Aunt Star and me. We all stood in silence like we were in an Old West standoff.

"Whatever." Karla turned and flounced toward the door.

"Wait a minute," I said as I followed her.

She turned as her long, slim fingers slipped around the door handle.

I tilted my head to the side. "What are you doing here?"

"What do you mean, 'What am I doing here?' I'm here for the reunion." She didn't say it, but I could hear her brain adding, "stupid," to the end of that sentence.

"What are you doing *at Jazzercise?*"

"I go at home, and I didn't want to miss just because I'm out of town." Karla and her husband lived in Kansas City. "Mom told me about this class, so here I am." She opened the door, and a blast of arctic air hit us. We hurried through to keep the cold air inside.

———

I SLEPT IN ON Saturday, as we had managed to get almost everything ready for the reunion on Friday, thanks to a little help from Aunt Star, Darren, and Trixie's husband Scott. I woke before my alarm but didn't get up. My curtains were closed, but the room was bright enough that I could tell the sun was shining, as the weatherman predicted. I closed my eyes and tried to go back to sleep, but instead I kept thinking about all the things on my to-do list for the day.

The alarm finally went off, ushering my day in with "Raspberry Beret." I sang along and used my fist as a microphone. When the song was over, I slid out from under the covers and padded over to my dresser.

I already knew what I was wearing to the reunion—a white skirt paired with a bright green silky blouse—but for now I needed something I could get sweaty in. I planned to put up some outdoor decorations at the fairgrounds, and the day was going to be a scorcher. I rifled through the dresser drawers and pulled out a pair of black knit shorts and an old Cherry Hill High

School Conference Basketball Champions T-shirt.

After finishing up at the fairgrounds the night before, we had all eaten dinner at The Blue Barn in downtown Cherry Hill. Aunt Star went to Darren's after we left the bar, and I hadn't heard her come home. I stuck my head out my bedroom door and saw that her door was closed, so I must have been sleeping deeply when she came in. Normally any little noise woke me.

I finished getting ready, grabbed a Diet Coke and a granola bar for breakfast, and opened the door into the garage. I reached up and hit the button to raise the overhead door before realizing Aunt Star's car wasn't in the garage. I froze. *If she's not home, who's in her bedroom?* A few seconds later I breathed a sigh of relief when my aunt's car came into view in the driveway. I still didn't move, though. Why would she have left her new sports car outside overnight?

The sound of the refrigerator door opening made me jump. I turned back toward the kitchen.

"Hey." Aunt Star stood in front of the open refrigerator. "You off to finish up?"

"Yeeeeah. Why is your car outside?"

"I know the garage door always wakes you up when I come home late, and you have a big day today, so I parked outside and came in the front door."

Aunt Star wasn't what one would consider to be a warm and thoughtful person, so the small gesture meant a lot. I crossed the kitchen and wrapped her in a hug. "Thank you."

She quickly extricated herself from my grasp and pulled an apple out of the fridge. She bit right into it, closed her eyes, and gave a small moan of pleasure. I took a step back and shook my head at her. I can't say fruit has ever made me respond that way, and especially not first thing in the morning.

She opened her eyes and saw my expression. "What? It's not weird. I love a cold, crisp apple."

"Whatever you say, weirdo." I headed back toward the garage. "I'll see you later."

"I've got a few house showings today, so I might not see you again before the reunion. Have an amazing time." She grinned. "And tell Mitchell hi from me."

I grinned back, waved, and closed the door behind me.

———

THE WOODEN SANDWICH-BOARD sign I dragged out to the fairgrounds entrance was not cooperating with me. The chain that kept the two sides from sliding apart had come loose from one side and I couldn't make the hook screw back into the wood.

"Need some help with that, Becky?"

I didn't need to turn around to recognize the man's voice.

"Billy Arbuckle!" I scrambled to my feet.

Billy opened his arms wide but then he dropped his left arm and stuck his right hand out for me to shake. I pushed it away and hugged him.

"What's wrong with you?" I asked with my head smashed against his chest. "Hugging is still allowed, even if you're married." And even if we had done a little more than hug each other in high school.

"Sorry." Billy let go of me and took a step back. He shrugged his narrow shoulders. "I didn't know if you'd be okay with it."

"And yes," I said begrudgingly, "I could use some help with this."

He laughed, as he well knew I hated letting people help me. I was a helper, not a helpee. With his assistance, the sign was set up in no time.

"I didn't think you could be here early," I said as we worked together to hang some streamers around the door of the 4-H Building. Billy was our class treasurer and therefore was on the reunion committee. "Didn't you have a wedding to attend in St. Louis today?"

"Yes, one of Paula's friends." Billy's wife Paula was also in our class. She and I were close throughout our childhood, but our friendship abruptly ended when the two of them had started dating after Billy and I broke up the summer before our senior year.

He continued, "But Paula and I got into a fight last night, and she refused to let me go with her today. I wasn't going to argue with getting out of going to a wedding, so I headed on out here. She'll come later. I just got to my parents' house," he motioned down the street where the Arbuckle house sat a block down, "and saw you out here working, so I thought I'd walk down and give you a hand."

"Thank you," I said. And I meant it. I was already sweating through my shirt.

He taped one end of a streamer to the top corner of the door. "Nice shirt, by the way."

"Brings back fond memories, does it?"

Billy had been the center on the conference champion basketball team our senior year.

"Some good, some bad. But mostly positive."

He didn't elaborate on the bad, but he was talking about Coach Banner. Coach was always hard on Billy, who concentrated much more on his grades than on basketball. That focus worked out for him, too, as he got a full-ride academic scholarship to Washington University in St. Louis and was now a successful financial advisor in the city.

"What have you been up to since you moved back to Cherry Hill?" he asked.

While we continued decorating, I told him about my job, living with Aunt Star, and Jazzercise.

"No boyfriend?"

"Technically no. But I do have a date for the reunion."

"Somebody I know?"

"No, he's a detective from Jeff City who came down to help with the investigation when Aidan Patrick was killed."

"I still can't believe that happened." Billy shook his head. "But a detective, huh? That's cool."

"In theory. But the primary part of his job is helping smaller police departments with major investigations, which means at any moment he could be called to another part of the state and might need to stay there for weeks."

"That's not great. Might not make for a stable relationship."

Honk!

We turned to the street as a car crunched toward us along the gravel entrance. I shaded my eyes with my hand and squinted at the black, two-door Mazda, but the sun's glare obscured the driver. The car parked and a slightly familiar-looking woman stepped out. Her long, blonde hair was teased to within an inch of its life, and she wore a hot pink cut-off t-shirt with an acid-washed denim miniskirt. My eyes traveled down her thin, tanned legs to a pair of pink stilettos.

Silence reigned while she stood before us with her hands on her hips.

Her identity finally came to me. "Anita Nichols, is that you?"

She grinned and nodded. My eyes opened wide. In high school Anita was kind and personable, but she was shy. She had dressed very conservatively, wasn't especially popular, and was never the center of attention. I hadn't thought she wanted to be. I must have been wrong. We *all* must have been wrong.

"It's awesome to see you!" I moved toward her. She met me halfway and gave me the briefest of hugs.

"I was driving by and saw you two, so I thought I'd stop and say hey. Hey!"

For the next several minutes, Anita peppered me with questions while the three of us completed the outside decorations. When we moved inside into the air conditioning, I went over my checklist one last time while Billy and Anita chatted at one of the tables.

I assured myself everything was ready and approached the duo, only to see Anita put her hand on Billy's and say, "I hope everything works out okay." She was struggling to keep a somber face. Was Anita interested in Billy? He wasn't the most handsome man, but he was successful. He was also married.

Billy didn't respond, but he also didn't move his hand out from under hers. I raised my eyebrows but neither of them noticed.

I interrupted their little moment with, "Everything's ready in here. Billy, thanks for your help. Anita, it's great to see you again." I shooed them toward the door. "I need to lock up here and head home to shower."

———

I RETURNED TO THE fairgrounds forty-five minutes before the official reunion start time, and four cars were already parked in the lot. A group of people stood around the building's entrance, impatiently waiting for the moment they could emerge into the coolness of the hall. As I walked from my car to the white metal building, I regretted my choice of silky shirt. Sweat was already forming along my spine.

I unlocked the door, and my former classmates nearly knocked me over in their rush to get inside. Before everyone could scatter to different areas of the room, I ensured they took their name tags from the table by the door. Several groaned at the senior photos attached to the tags, while others said they wished they still looked that good.

I put on my own name tag and hurried over to the boombox in

the corner that Darren and Scott had rigged up to some speakers. Aunt Star had loaned us her new player that would continuously play a tape from one side to the other without having to flip it around. I made sure my mixtape of songs from our high school days was completely rewound and hit play.

The opening sounds of "Hooked on a Feeling" blasted out of the speakers. The people nearby covered their ears until I got the volume turned down. I made a mental note to switch out the tape with a different one later in the afternoon. Then I retrieved pitchers of tea and a bowl of punch from the fridge and set them on the small counter between the kitchen and the main room, along with Styrofoam cups and a cooler full of ice.

As I made small talk, I kept one eye on the door, even though Mitchell had called earlier and said he wouldn't arrive until 3:30. I was disappointed he hadn't been able to meet me at my house so we could ride together, but at least he didn't need to cancel, which I'd been afraid of when he called.

The door opened and my heart leapt, even though I knew it couldn't be Mitchell yet. I sighed when Billy entered with Paula at his side. Not that I wasn't glad to see them, but they didn't quite compare to seeing Mitchell's toned body framed in the doorway. Neither of the two were smiling, so they apparently hadn't made up from their fight. I was also surprised they arrived early, since Paula had to drive a few hours from St. Louis after the wedding.

I crossed the room to the couple and asked Paula about their son. She perked right up and started telling me about three-year-old Zachary's latest accomplishments. Billy shot me a grateful look and slipped away to talk with some of the other guys.

A few more couples entered, and the female halves drifted our way, including Karla James Bright, who was no happier to see me than she had been on Thursday at Jazzercise. I soon found myself in a crowd where I didn't have a view of the entrance, so I excused myself from the group and crossed over to the door. I peeked outside, but the parking lot was quiet.

Standing alone by the door wasn't a viable option, but I didn't want to get into a long conversation and miss Mitchell's entrance. Thankfully, several of the new arrivals hadn't retrieved their name tags, so I gathered the tags up and circled the room to hand them out.

One of the tags belonged to Kyle Korte, who was currently rooming with Marty James, Karla's brother. As I approached, he looked me up and down and grinned. I immediately wished Mitchell was already by my side. The last thing I needed was to have to fend off the single men in the room, and especially one as annoying as Kyle. I was surprised he didn't have a date with him.

"Looking good, Becky. No date?"

"He's on his way."

Kyle's face briefly fell, but then he slapped a smile back on.

"Excellent." He paused. "I want to warn you that Karla's not happy with you."

"I know. I saw her on Thursday."

"I don't feel the same, you know. You were in a tough spot after Aidan died."

I nodded.

"Karla also has some beef with Billy, who we both know would never hurt a flea. Well, other than you." He shot me a grin and then scratched his chin. "I overheard her ranting to Marty about something to do with Billy, though I don't know exactly what."

"That's strange." I was afraid Kyle was going to want to keep chatting, so I said, "Sorry, but I need to go check on something. I'll talk to you later."

"Do what you need to do."

When I turned back toward the door, Trixie and Scott were

entering. I waved and hurried over.

"Mitchell here yet?" Trixie asked.

"Nope. He said he'd be here around 3:30."

Soon Trixie and I were deep into a conversation with Donna Daly Jenkins, who had been in choir and all the school plays with me. She still lived in Cherry Hill and taught at the high school, but our paths rarely crossed.

"What are you up to during summer break?" I asked her.

"Mostly hanging out at the pool and avoiding Jeff," she said with a smirk.

Donna married our classmate Jeff Jenkins a few years after high school, and they had recently gone through a nasty divorce. I chose not to respond to her comment about him.

"I haven't made it to the pool yet this summer. Today would have been a great day for it."

Two other women came up and joined the conversation, and I quietly slipped away. I headed toward the door to check the parking lot for Mitchell when a large group of people entered, and I was forced to step out of their way. The smell of alcohol wafted in with them, and a couple of the guys were toting cases of beer. A former linebacker on the football team carried a keg on his shoulder.

I sighed. We didn't have the budget to provide alcohol, so I made sure the invitations stated BYOB. If I hadn't, there would have been a revolt when people discovered only tea and punch. A few of the earlier arrivals brought six-packs of Bud Light and some Bartles & Jaymes wine coolers, and I had hoped that would be the extent of it. I should have known better. Things were likely to get rowdy fast.

Finally, I made it to the door and peeked outside. Trixie spotted me and shook her head.

"You keep watch for Mitchell," I pulled my lipstick out of my purse, "while I go freshen up. I'll be back in a jiffy."

I hurried across the room and down the hallway next to the kitchen. I pushed through the door into the ladies' room, and before I stepped over to the mirror, I noticed some lavender pumps below the wall in the last stall.

"Hey, Paula," I said, recognizing her shoes from earlier. The heels were the kind you could dye to match your outfit and were the exact shade of her dress.

The room was silent. I shot the feet a confused look but decided Paula must not like being disturbed while she was taking care of business. I studied myself in the mirror, moved a few curls back into place, and slicked on some more lipstick. Then I straightened the collar on my shirt and ensured I wasn't sweating through it anywhere.

Before exiting, I said, "I'll talk to you later, Paula," and was greeted with more silence. I shrugged and walked out.

Trixie stood by the door talking to Anita Nichols, who had kicked up her fashion another notch. She wore a tight leather miniskirt with a red, button-up blouse. Her front shirttails were tied together at her waist, leaving an inch of bare skin above her skirt. Above, enough buttons were left undone to announce to the world that she was wearing a lacy black bra.

I used every ounce of my strength to look her in the eyes. It wasn't my place to judge her for her wardrobe choices. I might not wear what she wore, but I would readily admit she confidently pulled it off.

I handed Anita her name tag, but she didn't have a place to put it considering the lack of material in her outfit. She halfway tucked it into a tiny, hidden pocket in her skirt.

The three of us struck up a conversation, and soon a hand touched the small of my back. I instinctively pulled away and turned, but instead of giving the person a piece of my mind, I squealed. Mitchell slipped a hand around my side, nudged me toward him, and kissed me on the cheek. I smiled at him, rested my hand on his bicep, and my fingers spontaneously gripped the solid muscle.

A hand snaked between us. "Hi. I'm Anita. And you are?"

Mitchell tore his eyes from mine, took a step back, and shook Anita's hand.

"Mitchell Crowe. Beckett's boyfriend."

I didn't know if he really considered himself my boyfriend or if he only said that to make a point to Anita, but I decided I was okay with it. I wasn't interested in dating anyone else.

Anita's forehead wrinkled. "Beckett?"

"Me." I pointed to my chest. "He's talking about me. I don't go by Becky anymore."

"I guess I assumed your name was Rebecca."

"Nope. It's Beckett—my mom's maiden name."

A scream echoed through the large room.

Mitchell's hand went to the waist of his khaki pants, as if going for a gun that wasn't there. While I stood stunned, he scanned the room in a split second and sprinted in the direction of the continuing screams.

THREE

AFTER A FEW SECONDS of confusion, I registered something big was happening, and I pushed my way through the excited crowd behind Mitchell. When I arrived at the hallway that led to the bathrooms, Mitchell's hands gripped Cheryl Young Stouffer's shoulders, and he gently but firmly asked her why she was upset. She couldn't speak but pointed down the hallway.

I started to head down the hall, but Mitchell's hand circled my wrist and pulled me back.

"Everyone stay back until I see what's going on," he ordered.

He strode down the hall, and someone yelled, "Who do you think you are?"

Scott's voice called out above the din, "He's a detective. Settle down, Dave."

The music abruptly stopped, someone pulled the now sobbing Cheryl back through the growing crowd, and everyone else tried to gather around the hallway entrance to watch. Trixie made her way to the front next to me.

Mitchell put his hand on the kitchen doorknob, and I held my breath. I didn't think anything could have happened in there, due to the pass-through window, but the entire space wasn't visible from the main room.

He attempted to push the door open, but something prevented it. He pushed harder, and the door flew open. Mitchell was silent for a moment before saying, "Carry on, but stay there," and he closed the door.

Trixie and I raised our eyebrows at each other. Then we returned our attention to Mitchell. He opened the door of the men's bathroom, glanced around, stepped into the room, and the door swung shut behind him. The crowd went silent.

I held my breath again, and the sound of slamming stall doors echoed down the hallway. I grabbed Trixie's hand and grasped it so tightly she gasped, but she didn't pull away. Mitchell reappeared, and I loosened my grip. He caught my eye for a second before continuing to the ladies' room. It was the only door remaining, other than the one leading outside at the end of the hall.

I suddenly recalled my one-sided conversation with Paula earlier, and nausea built up within me. Mitchell placed his palm on the door and pushed it open. His entire body tensed and then he let out a deep breath and disappeared into the room. My knees buckled, and Trixie yelled my name. A pair of strong hands caught me under the arms before I could hit the floor.

Mitchell shot back into the hall and raced toward me and Billy.

Billy said, "Sit down right here, Becky."

Mitchell reached us and helped settle me on the floor. He kneeled in front of me and put his hand under my chin. "You okay?"

"I will be. Just tell us what you found."

He studied me a few more seconds and then stood. He opened his mouth to speak, but then he held up a finger, took a few steps back, opened the kitchen door, and stuck his head in. "Come on out here, folks."

Kyle Korte emerged through the doorway, followed by Karla Bright. A ripple of whispers made its way back through the crowd. Kyle strutted toward us, but Karla had the grace to hang her head as she quickly walked up the hall. Kyle stopped next to me, while Karla avoided eye contact as she slipped away through the onlookers.

Mitchell finally addressed us. "I need everyone to go take a seat. Don't leave the building."

Nobody moved, but several people started asking questions at once, and Mitchell raised his hand. Shockingly, everyone quickly grew silent.

"I can't answer any of your questions right now." He looked at Trixie. "Can you go sit by the front door? If anyone tries to come in other than police officers or emergency responders, tell them they're not allowed to come in for the foreseeable future." Trixie nodded and slipped away.

Mitchell scanned the group and his eyes landed on someone behind me. "I need you to help me with something."

Scott was soon by my side. I wondered what Mitchell wanted him to do.

Then Mitchell helped me to my feet. "Where's the nearest phone?"

"Kitchen."

"Why don't you go wait with Trixie?"

I really wanted to stay right where I was or to help in some tangible way, but now was not the time to argue with him.

When I turned, most people were splitting off into smaller groups and pushing tables together to suit their needs. The volume swelled as everyone tried to guess what was happening. They all seemed to have forgotten that one person *did* know.

Though Mitchell had told me to wait with Trixie, I climbed up onto a chair to view the room. A few tables down, Karla and her husband whispered angrily at each other. In the far corner, several women huddled together at a table. I spotted Cheryl's black hair among them.

As I clambered back down off the chair, my bad leg buckled, and once again, Billy caught me.

"There we go." He helped me stand upright. "Did you see Paula while you were up there?"

I froze.

"What?" he asked.

I took a deep breath. "Nothing. No, I didn't see her. But I couldn't see everybody." I couldn't meet his eye. "Or maybe she stepped outside before all the commotion started." I shrugged and finally looked at him. He must have seen something in my eyes, because his body suddenly went rigid.

I took him by the arm. "Come with me."

Billy walked stiffly along beside me as I headed toward Cheryl. I grabbed a chair from another table and inserted it next to her. I sat, and Billy placed his hands on the back of my seat.

Cheryl stared straight ahead.

"She hasn't said a word," one of the other ladies said.

"Where's Randy?" I asked. Randy Stouffer, Cheryl's husband, was also one of our classmates.

"We don't know," said Donna Jenkins.

I took Cheryl's hand and squeezed it so tightly she turned toward me and slightly focused on my face. "Cheryl, I know this is hard. But what did you see?"

Her eyes finally cleared. Then she looked up at Billy behind me and broke down in sobs. Donna put her arm around Cheryl. The woman across from me caught my eye and then moved her eyes up to Billy. I turned and peered up at him. His normally pale skin was even paler, and he had a haunted look in his eye. I stood and steered him over to the door where Trixie was chatting with Anita.

Trixie's eyes widened when she saw Billy, and she pulled a chair over. I guided him into it, and he stared blankly at his hands.

Trixie bent her head next to mine. "What's going on?"

I spoke softly. "We can't find Paula."

Anita sidled up to us.

I continued, "I think she was in the bathroom earlier when I was in there, but she didn't respond when I tried to talk to her. I thought she simply didn't want to talk while she was in the bathroom."

Sirens sounded outside, and every person in the room turned their head toward the door. We waited silently, but nobody entered, so we went back to our conversations.

A minute later, Anita nudged me and jerked her head to the side. Across the room, Darren was closing the accordion doors on the kitchen counter. The drinks, ice, and cups were no longer in sight. Mitchell and Scott appeared in the hallway entrance. Mitchell stuck two fingers in his mouth and blew. The resulting whistle immediately stopped all conversation.

"Ladies and gentlemen," Mitchell said, "if you have any open drinks, please don't touch them. Leave them on the table, and an officer will come retrieve them. We'll give you more information in a moment."

The two men then crossed the room toward us. All heads followed them as they wound through the tables, and a few people grumbled about having their drinks taken away. The two men stopped in front of Billy and briefly looked at each other. Scott nodded, and Mitchell dropped to one knee. I placed my hand on Billy's shoulder and held my breath.

"Mr. Arbuckle," Mitchell began, and then cleared his throat, "I'm sorry to have to tell you this, but your wife has passed away."

I squeezed Billy's shoulder as tears streamed down my face and chatter erupted at the tables nearby. Billy closed his eyes and inhaled deeply through his nose.

He took a shaky breath. "What happened?"

Mitchell answered, "We're not entirely sure. Your wife may have died of natural causes, but we are strongly considering foul play."

Gasps rose from the crowd, though the statement shouldn't

have been surprising after the instructions about the drinks.

Trixie pulled a chair up on the other side of Billy and motioned Scott into it. He sat and awkwardly patted Billy on the back. Anita handed me a tissue and wiped her own eyes as the noise in the room grew louder.

Mitchell stood and faced the crowd, and the room quieted. "I'm sure you all heard that. None of you will be able to leave until we talk with you. You may be unsettled by the idea that your classmate may have been killed right here in this building, and that's understandable. However, we need your help to determine what happened."

"But the killer might be here in this room!" someone yelled.

"Maybe so, but I don't think they're going to try again in such a large crowd of people, with everyone on alert. Please be vigilant. We'll also keep an officer in the room at all times, and officers are stationed outside both doors. If you need to use the restroom, an officer will escort you to the men's room. You cannot use the phone. If you have an emergency, we're right here to take care of it. I doubt anyone expects any of you to be anywhere else for several hours at least, so settle in."

A few people complained, but since we had all planned to be in the building already, they couldn't really argue. Most people were in shock anyway, and a few women were sobbing. The attention shifted away from Mitchell and Billy, and everyone turned back to the people at their tables.

I checked my watch and realized the caterers would arrive in a half hour to set up the buffet dinner. I stepped away from Billy and put my hand on Mitchell's arm. He turned to me.

"The caterers will be here soon. What should we do? If we have to stay here, we'll need to eat. Plus, the food is already paid for."

He paused for a few seconds and then pointed at the door. "Officer Nichols is outside. The two of you can figure out a plan, but that plan must include not letting anyone in this room serve the food."

"What about drinks?" I spread my hands. "You're taking most of them away."

"I'd suggest finding a way to provide cans of soda. Individual drinks are the way to go. Don't do anything communal."

I nodded, and tears filled my eyes.

He reached up to wipe away a tear as it trailed down my cheek. "You okay?"

"No. Though Paula and I weren't close lately, we were as kids. But the thing is ..." I trailed off.

"What?"

"I maybe could have helped her."

He tilted his head. "How?"

"Was she in the last stall?"

"Yes. Well, kind of."

I wasn't sure what that meant, and I didn't really want to know. I shook my head to clear the vision that popped into my head. Then I told him about my earlier bathroom visit.

Mitchell sighed. "I'll need to take your official statement about that later. That encounter also means you're a witness. And, since you were alone in there with her, you're also technically a suspect—if this is a murder." His tone of voice confirmed he believed it was.

Trixie cleared her throat and narrowed her eyes at him. "You have *got* to be kidding me."

"I'm not." He sighed. "Do I like it? Absolutely not."

"But you don't think she's a murderer, right?"

Mitchell pressed his lips together before speaking. "As a police detective," he said with emphasis, "I'm not at liberty to say." He added under his breath, "In this setting."

Trixie and I both nodded.

"And with that in mind," he took a deep breath, "Trixie

should be the one to coordinate the food delivery."

I started to sputter a response, but he held up his hand and I stopped.

"Beckett," he said, not unkindly, "I can't be seen giving you special treatment, considering you're a—"

Trixie cleared her throat again.

Mitchell finished, "Uh, you know."

"*We know,*" Trixie said through gritted teeth.

He glanced between the two of us a few times and then gave me a look full of regret. I shot one right back at him. So much for him being my boyfriend. Nothing was going to happen on that front until this investigation wrapped up. I sighed and turned away from him. Though the situation wasn't his fault, I was still annoyed by it.

Anita said, "Officer ..."

"Crowe," he offered. *"Detective* Crowe."

I turned back to them.

"Detective Crowe," Anita said with a gleam in her eye, "if you're Becky's—I mean Beckett's—boyfriend, should you even be part of this investigation?"

FOUR

ANITA MADE AN excellent argument. *Say no, Mitchell!*

"That's a good point," he said, "but I overstated our relationship earlier. This was our first date. Also, in a small-town investigation, it's impossible for the officers and detectives to not personally know some of the people they're investigating." He pointed across the room at Darren. "In fact, Assistant Chief Turley probably knows Beckett better than I do." He pointed to the door. "As does Officer Nichols outside."

Anita nodded. "Officer Nichols knows me better than he knows Becky ... er, Beckett. He's my uncle Frank."

"I think you just proved me right," Mitchell responded. "And with that, I need to get back to the investigation. I'll talk to you ladies later." He headed toward the back of the building.

Scott shifted in his seat next to Billy and sent us a pleading look. It wasn't that Scott didn't care. He was a man of few words and even fewer outward emotions. Anita pulled Scott off the chair, slipped her arm around Billy, and murmured in his ear. I didn't think she was the best person to comfort him, but I couldn't very well take her place without causing a scene.

Trixie nodded toward the door, "I guess I don't need to stay here since Frank is out there."

"But you need to talk to him about the food."

She pursed her lips. "I don't understand why you can't do it. I don't know anything about the food, but you know everything."

"See if he'll come inside for a minute."

D.A. Wilkerson

Trixie stuck her head out the door and held a muffled conversation with Frank. Then she pulled back, and his head appeared through the slightly open door.

"Becky, I can't come in there unless another officer is out here, but I guess it won't hurt to talk to you from here. What do you need?"

I explained the food situation to him, and we worked out a plan. The caterers would set up on the sidewalk outside and plate the food for us. Then police officers would bring the plates in and place them at each person's seat along with a can of soda.

Meanwhile, Mitchell and Darren set up the kitchen as their temporary investigation headquarters. An officer collected all the open drinks from the tables and gathered up all the trash bags.

The police questioned Billy first. I felt bad for him, but I understood from my vast knowledge of fictional crimes that as the victim's spouse, he would be the primary suspect, if Paula hadn't died of natural causes. We didn't see Billy again after that. I wasn't sure what to make of his absence. Had the police let him leave to be with his and Paula's families, or did they take him to the police station?

In the main room, someone turned the music back on, but at a lower volume so as not to interfere with the interviews in the next room. A few people got up to dance, but when they realized nobody else was going to join them, they returned to their seats.

I wanted to talk to Trixie alone, so I pulled two chairs over by the name tag table. Quite a few tags had gone unclaimed. Some belonged to people who were present but hadn't taken their tag, but a handful contained names of people who weren't in the room. I wondered if they had changed their minds or if they arrived late and the police sent them away. If that were the case, what would they be thinking?

Trixie and I put our heads close together and spoke softly so we wouldn't be overheard.

She asked, "If Paula was murdered, do you think it was someone in this room?"

"Most likely. Why would anyone else chance being noticed, if they weren't supposed to be here? Anyone not at the reunion would have done it somewhere else."

"But why would anyone kill her here, where they might be seen, even if they're supposed to be here?"

I stuck my pinky nail between my teeth for a few seconds while I thought about my answer. "Maybe so there would be a lot of potential suspects. Or because they knew for sure she'd be here at a certain time, but they didn't know where else she might be or when."

"You think the killer planned it ahead of time?"

"There wasn't any blood—at least not that I could see when I was in the bathroom. It's hard to kill someone on the spur of the moment without any blood."

Trixie gave me a sharp look. "How do you know that?"

"Lots of Agatha Christie and *Murder, She Wrote.*"

"Oh." She paused. "I'm a little creeped out by the fact there's probably a murderer in the room."

"And that our old classmate is dead on the bathroom floor." I shivered, and tears pricked behind my eyelids.

"That, too."

"Which of our classmates is most likely to kill someone?" I asked.

"Hopefully none of them."

By the time the food arrived and everyone ate, the police had only interviewed about two-thirds of us, so we continued with some of my original plans for the evening to keep people's minds distracted from the reality of our situation.

We surveyed the attendees to discover who had come the farthest, who had been married the longest, and who had the most kids. I got out our senior yearbook and we reviewed the class superlatives—the people voted most athletic, most popular, most likely to succeed, and so on. This spurred a few stories, and we even shared some laughs together despite the overall somber mood.

Frank had been relieved of his outside duties and was given the task of calling the attendees back to the kitchen one by one. Trixie and Scott were among the last to take their turns, followed by Kyle, Karla, and finally Cheryl, who was somewhat recovered from her shock. I knew from experience, though, that she would continue to experience vivid flashbacks to the moment she found Paula's body. I still experienced them from when I found Aidan.

Finally, Darren appeared and asked me to wrap things up and send people home, after which he and Mitchell would interview me. I made the announcement, and most people headed straight to the door, but thankfully a few people stayed to clean up the mess we'd all left behind.

Trixie told me she'd oversee the work while I talked with the police. She also offered to call my family and let them know I was okay. I gave her a grateful hug, which she stiffly accepted with a few short pats on my back. My friend didn't love shows of affection.

I followed Darren back to the kitchen, where I recounted the events of the day since I arrived at the building in the morning. When I got to the part about Billy telling me he drove out early due to his and Paula's fight, Mitchell stopped me.

"You're saying Billy and Paula had a fight last night that was so bad she refused to allow him to go to a wedding with her, and he drove all the way out here without her?"

"Yeees." They should already know that, since they'd talked to Billy. Anita knew, too, and perhaps even others.

The two men briefly glanced at each other and then back at me.

"Is that news to you?" I glanced back and forth between them.

Darren cleared his throat. "We're not at liberty to say."

I rolled my eyes. "Come on, guys, it's me." I swept my arm from side to side. "There's nobody else here."

Mitchell sighed. "You know we can't tell you."

Everyone was silent for at least fifteen seconds.

"Okay, then," I relented. "I'll finish my story."

As expected, they asked many questions about when and where I saw Paula once she arrived at the reunion. Since I had been almost continuously checking my watch the entire time, waiting for Mitchell's arrival, I was able to provide accurate timing.

Though I knew they might not answer, one question was bugging me. "If all I could see was Paula's feet in the stall, why could Cheryl see more?" I wasn't sure I wanted to know how much more.

The two men looked at each other again. Mitchell gave Darren a slight nod.

"Our best guess is she remained upright on the toilet for a while, but then she toppled off," Darren explained. "There's no need for you to tell anyone that, though."

"I won't." I moved my gaze to Mitchell. "Why was it okay for me to know that but not whether you knew about Paula and Billy's fight?"

"One has to do with the facts of what you saw. The other has to do with motive."

I didn't know what any of that had to do with anything, but I let it go.

"All these questions make me think *you* think Paula didn't die of natural causes."

"She didn't have any health issues, according to Billy, so we're officially considering this a murder investigation."

"A poisoning, I'd guess, due to your food and drink rules."

Darren sighed and nodded at Mitchell. "We might as well tell her. She'll only make wild speculations if we don't."

"Hey! That's not nice!"

"It's true, though, isn't it?" Darren shrugged.

I couldn't disagree.

Mitchell said, "When I first saw Paula, I wasn't sure what had happened. There could have been many explanations. But when he showed up," he jerked his head toward Darren, "and inspected her closely, he said there was a faint smell of almonds."

My jaw dropped. "Almonds? She was poisoned with cyanide?"

Darren sat up straight. "Now how in the world could you know that?"

"Agatha Christie. She was always killing people off with poisons." I pointed at Mitchell. "You must not be able to smell cyanide. Not everyone can."

"I know," he replied.

"I wonder if I can." I cocked my head to the side as I pondered it.

Mitchell closed his eyes and shook his head. "Let's not try to find out."

"We'll need to get some testing done to prove it's cyanide, so don't share that information with anyone else just yet, okay?" Darren requested.

I mimed zipping my lips with one hand while crossing my fingers on the other hand under the table.

Darren pointed over his shoulder in the direction of the back door. "Did you unlock the back door when you arrived for the reunion?"

"No. I wanted everyone to come through the front so they could get their name tags. And when I left here this morning, I made sure it was bolted. That doesn't mean someone else didn't unlock it later, though."

"After we discovered the ... Paula's body," Mitchell said, "I checked the door, and it was bolted. That doesn't mean someone didn't unlock it in between, but it's unlikely. Nobody could have escaped out the door and locked it behind them unless they had a key."

Mitchell was from a small town, so he should know a building like this would have many keys floating around.

I said, "Who knows how many keys there are for this building, but the bolt on that door doesn't even have a keyhole on the outside. You can only lock it from the inside."

"Then I guess they didn't bolt it behind them," Mitchell said.

"They could have had an accomplice," I suggested.

"It's doubtful." Mitchell shook his head.

"You're right. Poisoning doesn't take two people, and with that being the case, why would you tell someone else you're going to commit murder?"

Darren reached over and placed a hand on the table in front of me. "You're getting a little too interested in this investigation. Do not—I repeat, *do not*—try to solve this murder. Remember what happened last time?"

"What? You mean me solving the murder?"

Darren sighed and slid his hand back to his side of the table. "No, I mean you putting yourself in a situation where you could have been killed, too."

"Oh, that." I shrugged. "Rookie mistake."

"Look me in the eyes," Darren commanded.

I leaned toward him and focused on his left eye, then his right eye, then his left again. I discovered it is practically impossible to look someone in both eyes at the same time, but I gave it my best shot.

Darren leaned across the table until our faces were inches apart. "Now tell me you are not going to try to solve this murder."

"I'm not going to try to solve this murder." I crossed my fingers again. I wasn't technically lying. The key word was *try*— I wasn't going to try, I was going to actually do it.

FIVE

WHEN I LEFT THE fairgrounds, I headed down the street toward Billy's parents' house to see if he was there. A late-model Honda Accord sat in the driveway, which I assumed to be Billy's, as I'd never seen it before. After a moment's hesitation, I whipped in and parked behind the Honda. I briefly wondered where Paula's car was.

I cut the engine and sat in silence for a moment, considering what I was going to say when I went to the door and wondering if I should simply leave. A movement caught my eye, and I turned my head to discover Billy's mom, Norma, leaning out the front door waving at me. Leaving was no longer an option, so I got out of the car. I stumbled on the top porch step, and she grabbed my arm and steadied me before I fell to my knees.

She then enveloped me in her arms before ushering me into the house, where a little boy was pushing a Matchbox car across the living room floor. The child was the spitting image of Billy.

Norma said to him, "Zachary, say hello to your daddy's friend Becky."

I didn't have the heart to correct her about my name.

Zachary looked up at me with an innocent smile. "'Ewwo, Becky."

My heart both melted and ached for him. He had no idea he would never see his mother alive again. I didn't even know if he was old enough to understand what death meant. I closed my eyes and breathed deeply. Norma steered me to the couch. I could hear her husband Elmer talking on the phone in the kitchen.

"Billy!" she called up the stairs. "Becky's here!"

To me, she said, "Would you like something to eat or drink? People have already started bringing food."

"Some water would be great. Thanks."

Footsteps sounded on the stairs, and Billy soon appeared. He held his arms open, and I pushed to my feet and stepped into them. He held me so tightly I could barely breathe, but I didn't have the heart to pull away.

"Stop squeezing the life out of that girl, Billy." Norma followed her statement up with a horrified, "Oh!"

Billy let go of me and gave his mom a side squeeze. "Don't worry about it, Mom."

Norma handed me a glass of ice water and motioned us toward the couch. I sat at one end, and Billy sank down beside me.

She crooked her finger at her grandson. "Zachary, come with Grandma for a moment."

"No!" Zachary continued playing with his car.

"I've got cookies," she said in a sing-song voice.

That did the trick, and the two disappeared into the kitchen.

Billy handed me a tissue from a box on the coffee table, and I wiped the tears from my cheeks. Then he placed his hand on my arm. "Are you okay?"

"The question is: are *you* okay?" I sniffled. "I'm so sorry."

I had never seen Billy cry, and today was no exception. His face was expressionless, and his eyes were now focused across the room. "I don't think it has really sunk in yet."

His hand was still on my arm, and I slowly moved out from under it. He didn't notice.

"Billy." I waited until his eyes shifted to mine. "Do you have any idea who could have done this?" I asked.

"No." He shook his head vehemently.

"Are you sure? Think hard. Has anyone been upset with her lately? Had she been in touch with anyone in our class?"

He stared out the front window, but I knew he was thinking.

"After Aidan died, Cheryl called her a few times."

I nodded. Cheryl and Aidan were cousins, and she was good friends with Paula in high school. It made sense Cheryl would call her old friend to talk through her grief.

"Did it ever sound like they were arguing about anything?"

"I was never home when they talked. Paula would just tell me Cheryl had called. She never said they argued, but since I didn't hear their conversations, I don't know for sure." He sighed. "I spend a lot of hours at the office. I'm not home much, so I don't know if she had talked to anyone else."

I wondered if Billy's absence was what the two of them fought about the night before. It wouldn't hurt to ask. "I know this is very personal, and you don't have to answer, but what did you and Paula fight about last night?"

His eyes cut to mine, and the corners of his mouth turned down slightly. "I'd rather not say."

"Okay. I get it. I shouldn't have asked."

A car door slammed outside. I didn't have a clear view of the entire street or the driveway out the window, so I didn't know if the person was coming to the Arbuckle house or not.

Ding-dong!

"Billy, can you get that?" his mother called.

His face was blank again. He hadn't registered the request. I stood and swung the door open to reveal Mitchell standing on the front steps. I doubted he was often visibly surprised while on the job, but shock filled his eyes.

"What are you doing here?" Mitchell asked.

"Checking on Billy. And you?"

"We need to ask him a few more questions. Couldn't get through on the phone."

"Yeah, his dad's been talking to someone the whole time I've been here."

We stared at each other for a moment. Mitchell raised his eyebrows.

"Oh! Come in."

He stepped inside.

"Who's there?" Norma bustled into the room while wiping her hands on a tea towel. She stopped short and cocked her head to the side. "I don't think I know you."

"Detective Mitchell Crowe." He stuck his hand out. She transferred the towel to her left hand and shook Mitchell's hand.

"Norma Arbuckle, Billy's mom."

"I'm sorry to intrude, but we need to ask your son a few more questions." He turned to Billy, who stared unblinkingly at us. Mitchell crossed the room, and Billy finally focused on him.

Mitchell said, not unkindly, "It'll be best if you come down to the station with me, sir. Shouldn't take long."

I didn't want to delay the investigation, so I quickly said my goodbyes and then drove directly to Trixie and Scott's house.

When Trixie let me in, I walked straight into the kitchen and picked up the phone. "I'm going to tell Aunt Star to come over. And I need to call my mom, or I'll never hear the end of it."

Trixie nodded and headed back into the family room. The house was quiet, as the kids were spending the night with her parents.

Aunt Star wanted all the details on the phone, but I wouldn't tell her anything, so she said she'd come right over.

My parents were in Chicago for a week visiting my brother Rafe's family, so I dialed his number and sat at the kitchen table. Though it wasn't her house, Mom answered the phone after only one ring. When she heard my voice on the line, she heaved a big sigh of relief.

"Your aunt called to tell me what happened, so I knew you

were okay, but I'm still glad to hear your voice. What if it had been you? I can't imagine what Georgia is going through right now." Mom was referring to Paula's mom, Georgia Olean. Paula's dad had passed away when we were in high school.

"Billy, too, and little Zachary."

"Yes. So, what happened?"

"I don't know many details, but the police are definitely saying it's murder." I shook my head, although she couldn't see me.

"How have there been two murders in Cherry Hill this year? I don't understand it."

"I don't either."

"Don't you dare try to solve this one." I could imagine Mom shaking her finger at me. "You stay out of it."

"Mom—"

"I mean it, Beckett Lee Monahan. Steer clear of this investigation. Promise me."

I couldn't even halfway lie to my mother about this. "You know I can't promise that."

She lowered her voice. "Well, if something happens to you, it's on your head then." She paused. "And don't you dare tell your father."

"I won't if you won't."

She snorted. "Not on your life."

We were both silent for a moment as we considered those words.

"I'll be careful, Mom. That's a promise I can make."

"I'll hold you to it."

She spent the next few minutes attempting to pull as much information out of me as she could, but I only gave vague answers. She finally let me go, but not after making me promise to keep her updated. Mom was very much afraid she would be out of the loop, especially since she wouldn't be at her job at the bank, where town gossip ran rampant.

Aunt Star had arrived while I was on the phone. She and Trixie were installed on the couch in the family room, and I made myself as comfortable as I could in an easy chair across from them. I wished I'd asked Aunt Star to bring me a change of clothes.

"Tell me what happened," Aunt Star said.

"Let me get Scott first." Trixie stood. "He can tell you two what he knows. He already told me, but it'll be more accurate coming from him firsthand."

She hollered down the stairs to Scott, who soon emerged from the basement. He plopped down in his brown leather recliner and cranked his feet up.

"I'll start," I said, "and tell you what happened before Cheryl found Paula." I began the sentence strong, but by the end I choked on the words and had to hold back tears.

Aunt Star pulled a tissue out of a box near her and handed it to me. "Take your time."

I took a few deep breaths to calm myself and then told them about my interactions with Billy and Anita earlier in the day.

"You don't know what Billy and Paula fought about?" Trixie asked.

"Nope," I replied. "I stopped by the Arbuckles' house on the way here and asked Billy. He wouldn't tell me."

"You've already started questioning suspects, huh?"

Aunt Star held a hand up. "Wait. Is Billy really a suspect?"

"The spouse is always a suspect," I explained. "Even more so when they've recently fought with the victim."

"Hmm. Good to know." Aunt Star tucked her feet under her. "How was Billy doing?"

"In shock, mostly."

"He's not the only one," Scott chimed in.

We all nodded.

"Was Anita really flirting with Billy this morning?" Aunt Star asked.

"It seemed like it to me," I said.

"She has really changed," Trixie stated.

"Indeed."

I continued my story and detailed my conversation with Paula, as well as our non-conversation in the bathroom.

"I guess she was already dead by that point." I felt like I was going to throw up and raised my hand to my mouth.

"Are you all right?" Aunt Star came over and knelt beside me.

"I need some water."

Trixie disappeared into the kitchen and came back with a glass of ice water. "Do you want me to talk for a while?"

I nodded, and Aunt Star returned to her seat.

"I had a brief conversation with Paula, too," Trixie said. "She told me she'd gone to a friend's wedding this morning, but she didn't say Billy didn't go with her or that they drove separately."

"Who has a wedding in the morning?" Aunt Star asked.

"Seems like you wouldn't have enough time to get ready," I replied.

Trixie ignored our comments. "Paula made a not-so-nice comment about Anita, but now that I think about it, Anita hadn't even arrived at the reunion yet. That's odd."

I perked up at that statement. "That must mean something, right? She must have seen Anita somehow, because nobody would have anything bad to say about the Anita we used to know."

"I didn't think to tell Darren and Mitchell about it." Trixie bit her lip.

"We can come back to that later," I said. "Let's keep going. Scott's falling asleep on us."

I pointed at the man in question, who was lying all the way back in his recliner. He raised a finger in acknowledgment.

"Anita came up to me while you were in the bathroom." Trixie nodded at me. "We chatted for a minute before you got back. And then Mitchell came in."

Aunt Star raised her hand again. "Forgive me, but with all the excitement, I completely forgot about Mitchell. What happened there? I guess he's now involved in the investigation."

I spread my hands. "Nothing happened. We had barely said hello when Cheryl started screaming, and he immediately took charge. We all ran over to see what happened. Cheryl couldn't even speak, so Mitchell was forced to find out on his own. That's when he found Paula in the bathroom. Well, we didn't know that for sure at first, but I had a feeling."

"That's why you almost passed out," Trixie said.

"Yes."

"And guess who else Mitchell found while he was searching," I said to Aunt Star.

She shrugged.

"Karla and Kyle were together in the kitchen!"

Aunt Star's eyes opened wide. "No."

"Yes. Kyle had been flirting with me not a half hour earlier, but when he found out I had a date, he backed off. Didn't take him long to move on." I paused. "He did say something interesting, though. He told me Karla was mad at me about Marty, which I knew. But he also said Karla had some issue with Billy, though he didn't know what."

"Who would have an issue with Billy?" Scott chimed in. "Everybody loves that dude."

"Apparently Becks had an issue with him years ago, or she wouldn't have broken up with him." Aunt Star gave me a pointed look.

"Water under the bridge." I shrugged. "That was a long time ago."

Trixie caught my eye, and I quickly looked away. I wasn't

going to get into that story at the moment.

"Your turn, Scott," I said. "What happened after Mitchell sent us back to our seats?"

Scott sat up so he could see us better. "He needed someone to identify her. He didn't know many people there, and I guess he figured I could handle it better than you girls could."

"I could have handled it fine!" Trixie exclaimed.

She definitely could have dealt with it better than Scott or me, but Mitchell didn't know that.

"And I'm not a girl," she added with a glare at her husband.

"Sorry. You're a woman."

She gave him a brisk nod.

"Anyway ..." I prompted Scott.

"Are you sure you can handle the details?" he asked.

We nodded in unison.

"She was on the floor, with her top half outside the stall and her body partly angled toward us. Her hair was a little bloody, like she'd hit her head on the wall or floor or something. And there was vomit on her mouth and dress. The worst part was ...," his Adam's apple bobbed a few times before he could continue, "her eyes were open." He closed his own eyes. "I'll never get that image out of my head."

"Oh, babe," Trixie got up and perched on the arm of his chair.

Scott pulled her into his lap, wrapped his arms around her, and buried his face in her neck. Aunt Star and I both looked away while he composed himself. I felt a rush of anger toward Mitchell for putting Scott through that. Surely he could have waited for a local police officer to identify the body.

To take the focus off Scott, I filled Aunt Star in on the rest of the story.

Trixie was still on Scott's lap, but his arms were now loosely draped around her.

I asked them, "Did you find out anything else when they

questioned you?"

They both shook their heads.

"I'm not supposed to say what I learned from them," I said.

Everyone stared at me expectantly. They knew I'd cave.

"Okay, fine. Since you insist, I'll tell you. First, I'm pretty sure they didn't know about Billy and Paula's fight until I mentioned it."

"That doesn't look good for Billy," Trixie said.

"No. And the other thing is they're almost certain she was poisoned."

"Poisoned!" Aunt Star repeated.

"With cyanide," I added.

"Holy smokes." Trixie sat up quickly.

"Oof!" Scott shielded his ribcage with his hands.

Trixie apologized for elbowing him and we all sat in silence for a moment.

"No wonder Mitchell made those strict rules about our meal," Trixie said.

"Yep. I'm kind of surprised he let us eat at all," I replied.

"When the police took all the open drinks, that should have tipped everyone off that they thought it was poison," Scott said.

"I thought it was some weird crime scene thing." Trixie's eyes narrowed and she turned to face her husband. "You knew." She pressed her finger into his chest. "You knew she was poisoned, and you didn't tell me!"

Scott picked at a loose thread on the arm of his chair. "The cops told me not to tell anyone." He shrugged and finally looked his wife in the eye. "What can I say? You know I'm a rule follower. Unlike others in the room."

All eyes turned to me. I held my palms up.

"So how does somebody get their hands on cyanide?" Aunt Star asked. "And how did nobody else get sick or die?"

Brrrring!

Trixie stepped into the kitchen to answer the phone. Shortly after, she popped her head around the doorway and looked at me. "It's for you."

I raised my eyebrows. "Me?"

She held her hand over the mouthpiece. "It's Mitchell."

SIX

I UNFOLDED MY LEGS from under me and stumbled when I stood, as my bad leg was asleep. I made my way into the kitchen and took the phone from Trixie.

"Hello?"

"Hey. You okay?"

I was still irritated with Mitchell for involving Scott, and I was tempted to tell him so, but I didn't think it would be helpful for any of us at this point. I also didn't want him to know Scott had told us the details, so I simply answered, "Not really, but I'll be fine."

"You sure?"

"Yes. How are things going there? Are you done questioning Billy? Where are you? How did you know where to find me?"

"That's a lot of questions, but I'll try to answer them all. Things are fine. We've sent Billy back home—or I guess to his parents' house. I'm calling from Chief Dover's office, because he's on vacation this week. I tried calling your house, but I didn't get an answer, so Darren said I should try Trixie's."

"Ah." I leaned against the kitchen counter and twirled the phone cord around my finger. "Are you getting anywhere with the investigation?"

"Beckett ..."

"I know. You can't tell me."

We were both silent for a few seconds.

"Can you tell me if I'm going to be able to see you?" The end of my finger started to turn purple, so I unwound the phone cord from it.

"We can't be seen together in town. When we were interviewing your friend Anita, she brought up our relationship again."

"I don't know what her deal is. She was so kind and friendly in high school. Now she's ... I don't know. Different."

"Different how?" His voice took on a more professional tone. He was shifting into detective mode.

"She dresses differently, for one. I don't really care what she wears, but she used to be much more conservative in the way she dressed. And she was always quiet and shy. She was never the center of attention, and she didn't seem like she wanted to be. Oh, and there's another thing. Trixie talked to Paula before she died, and Paula said something negative about Anita. I don't know what she said, but Anita hadn't arrived at the reunion yet, so it was strange that Paula was talking about her."

"Do you know if the two had kept in touch?"

"Sounds like they had. Otherwise, I don't know why Paula would have said anything, especially because I can't think of anything from high school that Paula would have been upset about now."

"I'll need to talk to Trixie about what Paula said."

"Do you want me to put her back on the phone? Or you could come over here," I suggested. It might be okay for us to see each other in a group.

He paused. "I could maybe do that."

"Aunt Star is here, too." I thought it might help matters if even more people were present.

"Hold on a second." The line crackled as he covered the receiver with his hand and held a muffled conversation. "Okay," he said to me, "Darren and I are both coming over. That way it won't be my truck in the drive. We have a few more questions for you and Scott, too."

We said goodbye, and I headed back into the family room, where nobody was saying a word. I stopped short. "Did you hear that whole conversation?"

They all nodded.

"Darren is coming, too."

Aunt Star ran her fingers through her hair. I don't think she even realized she did it.

"They want to ask us a few more questions." I settled back into my chair. "He wants to hear what Paula said about Anita."

"What *did* she say?" Aunt Star asked.

"She called Anita a word I won't repeat and said she needs to mind her own business."

I frowned. "What's that about?"

Trixie shrugged.

Mitchell and Darren soon arrived. Darren sat in one of the kitchen chairs Scott brought into the living room, and Mitchell stood behind the other chair. My belly did a flip at the sight of him, still wearing his dress clothes from the reunion. He gave me a searching gaze, and I smiled at him. His eyes softened, and he smiled back.

"We should talk to Trixie in another room," Mitchell said.

I decided to bite the bullet. "We've all already told each other everything we know." I took a deep breath. "Even about the cyanide."

"Beckett!" Darren objected.

"Sorry, but you can't tell me you didn't know I'd tell Aunt Star and Trixie. I don't keep any secrets from them."

Mitchell raised his eyebrows at that declaration.

"Well, not about stuff like this, at least," I amended, with a glance in his direction. Though I told them almost everything about him, too. Best to leave him in the dark about that.

Mitchell took a seat, pulled a small notebook and pen out of his pocket, and asked Trixie about her conversation with Paula.

"Did she say anything else about Anita?" he asked after Trixie relayed what Paula said.

"No. I mentioned that Beckett told me she saw both Billy and Anita this morning. She didn't look happy about that, but she didn't comment on it."

Darren turned to Scott. "Did you talk to either Paula or Anita this afternoon?"

"I didn't see Anita until after all the commotion. I said hi to Paula, but I didn't have a conversation with her." His forehead wrinkled. "I did see her holding a cup of punch, though."

Mitchell's eyebrows slightly raised at that revelation. "Do you remember when that was?"

Scott pressed his lips together while he thought. "Not too long before Cheryl found her. Ten minutes? Twenty, tops."

"Can cyanide work that fast?" Aunt Star asked.

"If it's highly concentrated, it can work in minutes," Mitchell explained.

"How would somebody get the poison into only her drink?" Trixie inquired. "And how do you get cyanide in the first place?"

"We're still working on all of that." Darren clicked his pen a few times. "We don't even know for sure it was in her drink. The autopsy report and lab results on the drinks we collected should help, but since it's the weekend, that will take a few days."

If I knew Trixie, she'd be at the library first thing Monday morning learning everything she could about the poison.

Mitchell asked, "Is there anything else you told each other that you didn't tell us? Or did you have any other interactions with Paula or Billy?"

Trixie raised her hand. "I chatted with Billy for a few minutes. He talked about Zachary and said he works long hours. That's about it."

Darren pointed at me. "Detective Crowe said you were at

Billy's house. Did he tell you anything relevant?"

I told them the details of our brief conversation, and both men took notes.

"One other thing," I said. "Anita didn't arrive at the reunion until I was in the bathroom … you know, when Paula was in there. She was talking to Trixie by the door when I came back out."

"No, she had been there for a little while," Trixie corrected me. "Maybe five or ten minutes."

Mitchell flipped his notebook closed. "I think we're done here." He inclined his head toward me. "Is there someplace we can talk for a minute?"

I looked at Trixie, who motioned toward the hallway. Mitchell followed me down the hall, and I turned into Krystal's bedroom, flipped on the light, and closed the door behind us.

Mitchell took in the eight-year-old's room with a grin. "My niece loves Strawberry Shortcake, too." The curtains and comforter on her canopy bed featured the popular character, and various other dolls and toys dotted the room.

He crossed to the window and pulled down the shade. It shot right back up, and he yanked it down again. Then he grasped my waist and pulled me to him. As I gazed up into his eyes, my heart pounded with anticipation.

"We've been waiting months for this, so I'm going to kiss you one time, and that has to be it until this investigation is over," he declared.

I wrapped my arms around his neck, and he lowered his lips to mine. An indeterminate amount of time later, a burst of laughter from the family room pulled us back to reality. Mitchell untangled his fingers from my hair, and I stepped back, took several deep breaths, and gripped a post at the end of Krystal's bed to steady myself. Mitchell stuck his thumbs into his belt loops and leaned against the door.

I pointed to my lips and then to him. "You've got some lipstick on your mouth." I didn't trust my legs to carry me over to wipe it off for him.

"You don't think it looks good on me?" He grinned, stepped over to the white, wicker-framed mirror above Krystal's dresser, and swiped the back of his hand across his mouth a few times. He then took my hand and pulled me over to the mirror. "You might want to use this, too." I smiled at the sight of us together, and then I noticed my hair, which was a complete disaster.

I reluctantly let go of his hand and attempted to put my curls back into some semblance of order. "Are we allowed to even talk on the phone?" I looked at him through the mirror.

He picked up a small, stuffed Care Bear from the dresser and tossed it from one hand to the other while he considered my question. I couldn't help but smile at the sight.

"Yes, but we can't talk about the case. And I'll have to call you."

I nodded as I smoothed my hands down over my hair. He was staying at The Oak Street Hotel—known to locals as The Osh—and all incoming calls were routed through the front desk. I wouldn't be able to call him there without someone knowing, and I also couldn't call him at the police station.

"If you need to call the station for any reason, ask to speak to Darren or Frank, not me." He set the stuffed animal back down.

"Speaking of the station, I'm guessing someone has told you Cheryl Stouffer is Barbara Young's daughter." Barbara ran the front desk at the Cherry Hill Police Station on weekdays.

Mitchell sighed. "Nobody thought to mention that. Thanks."

"I guess everyone assumes everyone else knows these things in a small town."

"Any other family connections I should know about?" He twirled a finger through one of my curls.

I swatted his hand away and gave my hair a final pat. "Let's go back out and we can all fill you in."

"After you." He opened the door and swept his hand toward the hallway.

His fingers grazed the small of my back as I passed him, and all the hair on my arms raised to attention.

"You have a nice *talk?*" Aunt Star's mouth twitched.

I felt the blush running up my chest. "Um, yes. Hey, I mentioned to Mitchell about Barbara being Cheryl's mom. He wants to know all the other connections that might be helpful in the investigation."

"Sorry I didn't think to tell you that," Darren said to Mitchell.

"No problem. We've had other things on our minds."

Aunt Star stifled a laugh.

I glared at her and then turned my focus to Mitchell. "Get your notebook back out. Karla Bright, who you found in the kitchen with Kyle Korte?"

Mitchell nodded and clicked his pen.

"First off, she's married, if that didn't come up while you questioned her. Her husband was there, but I don't remember his name. He's not from here. Secondly, she's Marty James' sister."

"The Marty who caught you poking around his shed back in March?"

"That's the one. He runs the hardware store downtown. And Kyle Korte is his roommate. It's Marty's house, but Kyle has been rooming with him for a while. Oh! And Kyle told me Karla was upset with Billy about something, but he didn't know what. He overheard her talking to Marty about it."

Both policemen scribbled notes.

"Anita told you she's Frank's niece," I said to Mitchell, who nodded.

Trixie said, "Cheryl's husband, Randy Stouffer, was also in our class, but he wasn't there today." She looked at me. "Do you know why?"

"Nope."

Scott offered, "I ran into him at the Dairy Queen earlier this week and he said he'd see me at the reunion."

"I saw him this morning," Aunt Star said. "He was getting his truck filled up at McCoy's when I was there." McCoy's 66 gas station sat at the four-way stop in downtown Cherry Hill, catty-corner from First Comm. The full-service station was owned and operated by Trixie's dad, Marvin McCoy. "Didn't talk to him, but he appeared to be fine."

"Does Paula have family in town?" Mitchell asked.

"Only her mom," I said. "She has a brother, but he lives in Arkansas. Her dad died when we were juniors." I frowned. "I hope somebody's with Georgia. Billy and Zachary were both at his parents' house."

"Veronica's over there," Aunt Star said.

My pastor's wife and Georgia were very close, so that made sense. What didn't make sense was my aunt knowing Veronica's whereabouts.

"How do you know that?"

"She called me from there," Aunt Star said.

"What?" My forehead wrinkled. "Why?"

"Veronica and I talk."

"Since when?"

"Since you two almost got yourselves killed together."

"Oh."

That reasoning held up, but my aunt and Veronica both had very intense, take-charge personalities, so I was surprised they got along. Until Veronica and I worked together to solve Aidan's murder, I didn't think the two women had even talked to each other in the ten years the Cokers had been at First Comm. Aunt Star wasn't a churchgoer.

Mitchell tapped his pen on his notebook. "Anything else?"

"Billy has older twin sisters, but they don't live around here,"

Darren said. The twins were in Darren's class—either '68 or '69, I couldn't remember which.

Darren slipped his notebook and pen back into his shirt pocket and stood. "Thanks for all your help, folks. Let us know if you think of anything else." He looked pointedly at me and then the others. "And please don't say anything to anyone about the cyanide for now."

We all agreed.

"But," I added, "the people who were at the reunion are probably going to guess it was poison, considering you took everyone's drinks and didn't let us set up the buffet."

"True, but they won't know what kind of poison, which makes a difference."

The two policemen left, and then Scott said goodnight to us and headed down the hall. I looked at my watch. I had registered that darkness had fallen, but I didn't realize it was almost 10:00.

I started to get to my feet, but Aunt Star held a hand up. "Not so fast, missy."

I let myself fall back into the chair. "What?"

"Did you do more than talk back there with Mr. Detective? Was there any *investigating* going on?"

Trixie snorted and grinned. My chest and face heated again.

"Ha!" my aunt said. "I thought your hair was a little messier than before."

"We only kissed. Once. He said that's all that can happen until the investigation's over."

"You were back there a long time for one kiss." Trixie raised an eyebrow.

"What can I say?" I smirked at them. "We took advantage of our one chance. And we did briefly talk."

"About what?" Trixie wasn't normally nosy, but when it came to my love life, she wanted all the details.

"About how we can't see each other. And we probably won't

even be able to talk on the phone much. But if we do, it can't be about the case."

"You're not going to want to talk about anything *but* the case until it's solved, though," Aunt Star said.

"Too right." I sighed. "But we'll make it work."

"Remember how we joked about needing another crime to get Mitchell back to town?" my aunt asked.

"Yep, and I had hoped for a bank robbery—not a murder. Though since Mom works at a bank, I guess I don't want a robbery, either. I never dreamed we'd have another murder, and what are the odds I'm a witness *again?*"

"Pretty low." Trixie was probably figuring the percentages in her head.

Brrrring!

"Who'd be calling at this time of night?" She hopped up and headed into the kitchen to answer the phone. "I hope the kids are all right."

Aunt Star and I stayed silent so we could eavesdrop.

"Hello? ... Sorry, I can barely hear you," Trixie was silent for a moment. "Uh-huh. ... Yeah, she's here. ... We'll see. ... Yeah, thanks."

"What was that about?" Aunt Star inquired when Trixie re-entered the room.

"That was Donna Jenkins calling from The Blue Barn. A bunch of our classmates are up there if we want to join them."

I sighed. "I'm tired, but I'm not going to pass up a chance to find out everything I can about what happened today. Anyone else in?"

"I'm out." Trixie looked at Aunt Star. "Unless you can't go. I don't want her to go alone."

"I'm happy to be her chaperone," my aunt said. "There's nowhere I need to be, since Darren will likely be at the station all night. I doubt I'll see much of him for the next several days."

"Hopefully he'll be able to make time for you on your birthday, though," I said.

My aunt was a July Fourth baby, and the holiday was coming up on Thursday.

"Even if the investigation isn't still going strong at that point, it's all hands on deck for the police department on the holiday."

That made sense, with the town parade that morning and thrill-seekers losing fingers to fireworks later in the day.

Aunt Star pushed off the couch. "If we're going to do this, let's get on with it."

SEVEN

WE STOPPED BY THE house on the way to the bar so Aunt Star could change clothes and I could freshen up. I touched up my lipstick and eyeshadow, added more hairspray, and traded my pumps for the green jelly shoes Aunt Star had given me for my birthday.

Soon we were on our way to The Blue Barn. The street parking was full, so we parked in First Comm's lot.

Contrary to its name, the bar was housed on the first floor of a two-story red brick building that looked much like the others along Main and Oak Streets in downtown Cherry Hill.

The bar was standing room only, and one of my classmates must have taken control of the jukebox, because instead of recent Top 40 or country hits, "Kung Fu Fighting" was blaring from the speakers. I anticipated more songs from our high school days were to come. I was surprised there was no live music, as the bar typically hosted local bands on the weekends.

We squeezed between tables and made our way over to the bar, where we stopped next to Kyle Korte and Randy Stouffer.

"Randy!" I said over the noise. "How's Cheryl doing?"

He moved his head closer to my ear so I could hear him clearly. "Donna brought her home, and she went straight to bed. She wouldn't talk about it."

"I feel so bad for her," I said. "By the way, where were you this afternoon?"

He leaned back away from me. Aunt Star and Kyle had been

chatting, but they stopped when I asked the question. I raised my eyebrows at Randy. He let out a deep breath and we all leaned toward him.

"Her parents picked the kids up, and we were ready to leave when I got a call from Jock Feamster that some of his cattle were out on the highway. He asked if I could help round them up." He stuck his hands in his jeans pockets and looked at the ground for a moment. "I know I should have said no, but I didn't. I told Cheryl to go on to the reunion without me, and I'd be there as soon as I could. But by the time I got there, the cops had the place surrounded. They wouldn't even tell me what happened. I'll tell you, I was worried."

I briefly touched his arm. "I bet you were. Were you able to find out what happened before Cheryl got home?"

"I went straight home and called Suzanne LaHaye. I figured if anybody knew what was happening, it would be her."

We all nodded. Suzanne LaHaye was the worship leader at First Comm and a vital branch of Cherry Hill's grapevine.

"She heard the news from Veronica Coker." He shook his head. "I couldn't believe it. Who would want to kill Paula?"

Anita suddenly inserted herself between Kyle and Randy. She held a martini glass in one hand and slid a hand around Randy's arm with the other. Aunt Star and I caught each other's eyes but quickly focused back on Anita. She didn't notice because she was gazing up at Randy. After a few awkward seconds, he took a small step back and her hand dropped from his arm.

"Hey, watch it!" came a shout from behind him.

Randy moved to the side, and Jeff Jenkins turned to face us, while shaking beer off his hand.

"Sorry, man," Randy said. "Let me buy you another one."

"Don't worry about it," Jeff clapped a big hand on Randy's shoulder. "It's been a rough day all around, huh?" Jeff had been the vice-president of our class. He and Randy were athletic rivals in high school, but since Jeff's ex-wife Donna and Cheryl were close, the men had become friends as adults.

"Becky, Starla," Jeff said, "can I buy you a drink?" He swept his hand toward Kyle and Randy. "Since these two Neanderthals apparently haven't offered to get you one."

Randy's face turned red, and Kyle sputtered out, "Hey, they haven't been here all that long!"

"That's true. And yes, I'd like a Bud Light. Thanks." I didn't typically drink alcohol, but it wasn't a typical night.

Aunt Star asked for a glass of the house red wine, and Jeff pushed his way to the bar. As I followed his progress, I spotted Donna further down the bar talking to Marty James. I wanted to go ask Marty why Karla was upset with Billy, but I also wanted my drink, so I decided to wait a few minutes.

Since I had my suspicions about Anita, I didn't want to ask anyone in the group anything about the murder, so I asked Anita how long she'd be in town.

"I'll be here all week. I'm spending Monday on the lake with some friends, and I also promised Mom I'd help her with the parade float." Anita's mom ran a daycare in town, and she always entered an elaborate float in the Fourth of July parade.

"Local friends or Columbia friends?" I asked, referring to her comment about spending Monday on nearby Lake of the Ozarks.

"St. Louis friends."

My eyebrows shot up. The last I knew, she lived in Columbia.

"I moved there right after Christmas. I can't believe you didn't know that."

I couldn't believe it either.

Jeff returned with our drinks, and I made a few more minutes of small talk before excusing myself from the group and making my way over to Donna and Marty. Aunt Star followed me, but she got waylaid along the way by a couple she was helping with a house sale. I sang along to "The Joker" as I squeezed between groups of my former classmates, hoping none of them would stop me.

"No Trixie?" Donna asked around a cigarette when I reached her side.

"You know her. Not a late-night person on the best of days, and this is not one of those days."

Donna nodded. "When the teachers go out, she's always the first to leave."

I greeted Marty and then, since I knew at any time our group of three could turn into a group of five or more, I started right in with my questions.

"How was Cheryl doing when you left her?" I asked Donna.

"Not great. I mean, can you imagine?" She grimaced. "Oh, I guess you can."

"Yeah, not fun."

"Do you know if she kept in touch with Paula?" The two were inseparable during our senior year, so I imagined she had.

"They used to talk every few weeks, but lately it's been more like a few times a year." She flicked her cigarette ashes into an ashtray on the bar. "I haven't talked to Paula in a while. Jeff and I used to meet Billy and her for dinner when we'd be in St. Louis. Of course, that's been a few years. Anyway, Cheryl talked to her a couple weeks ago. She told me Anita had been over to Billy and Paula's house a few times. Pretty weird, since they were never really friends."

Yes, it was weird, but that partly explained why Paula made a comment about Anita to Trixie. What was also strange was Billy had acted like he didn't know who Anita was when she arrived at the fairgrounds that morning. Though once I thought about it, I realized he didn't say he didn't know her, but he also didn't help me out when I didn't initially recognize her.

"Did she say anything about Anita or only that she'd been to their house?"

"Paula wasn't very happy about it. Anita always made the plans through Billy."

"Interesting."

Donna blew out a cloud of smoke that drifted in Marty's direction. He coughed and waved the smoke away and my focus shifted to him. He was leaned back against the bar and hadn't said a word during my conversation with Donna.

I said to him, "I heard your sister isn't happy with Billy for some reason."

"Karla isn't happy with most people." He took a swig from his beer bottle.

"Care to enlighten us about her problem with Billy?"

"Why?" His mouth twitched. "So you can suspect her of murder, too?" He cocked an eyebrow at me.

I didn't know whether to laugh or apologize. Instead, I took a sip of my beer and choked on it. Marty reached around and lightly whacked me on the back, which made me stumble into Donna, who kept both of us from falling to the floor.

Marty pulled a stool out from under the bar and helped me climb onto it. It took me several seconds to figure out how to sit on it in a ladylike position in my skirt. Marty watched with amusement.

Donna pointed her cigarette at Marty but looked at me. "Did you suspect *him* of Aidan's murder?"

I hung my head. "I hate to admit it, but yes." I glanced back up at Marty. "Are you going to answer my question?"

"I'm considering whether or not it would be good for your health," he teased.

"While you consider that," Donna turned to me, "I want to know more about Detective Dreamy." She batted her eyelashes. "The man sure knows how to take charge of a situation."

Marty leaned back on his heels. "What's this about, Miss Monahan?"

"She's talking about Mitchell Crowe, my date for the reunion. Did you meet him when he was here helping with Aidan's investigation?"

Marty shook his head.

"Today was our first official date, and it lasted all of two minutes before he was forced to switch to detective mode. And now, since I'm a witness, I can't even see him." I decided not to mention I was also a suspect.

I finished off the last of my beer. Marty took the bottle from me and set it and his own empty bottle on the bar. He called to the bartender to bring us another round.

"One's all I can handle," I said. "I don't need another."

"Yes, you do, honey." Donna smashed her cigarette stub into the ashtray behind me. "Let the man buy you a beer. He's celebrating getting a new truck, so he's feeling generous. I can drive you home if need be."

"Aunt Star drove us," I said, and at that moment my aunt joined us.

"I thought I'd never get away from them," she said.

Donna craned her neck in the direction Aunt Star had come from. "Who?"

"The Cordells. I'm selling their house."

"Where are they going?" Donna asked.

"Somewhere up near Kansas City."

I cut in before they could get into a long conversation. "Marty was about to tell us why Karla's mad at Billy."

Marty handed me my new beer. He motioned to Aunt Star. "You want something?"

"Some ice water. I'm driving."

Marty asked the bartender for a water and turned back to find all three of us staring at him.

Donna lit another cigarette. "You might as well tell us. It's going to seem very suspicious if you don't."

The woman made a compelling point.

Marty pursed his lips and pretended to think for several seconds before saying, "She called Billy a few months ago to ask his opinion on an investment her husband was about to make. Billy told her since he wasn't their advisor, it wasn't his place to say. I think there was also a legal reason. Anyway, Chip made the investment, and it tanked. You didn't hear this from me, but they lost almost everything."

"Ouch." Though I didn't like Karla, I felt bad for her. "That's not Billy's fault, though."

"No, but you know my sister."

Aunt Star, Donna, and I all nodded.

The alcohol had loosened me up enough that I asked Marty, "Did you hear where she was when Cheryl found Paula?"

"Beckett ..." my aunt warned.

I blushed a deep red. "Sorry, Marty, I was out of line. Ignore me."

He gave my shoulder a pat. "Don't worry about it. I did hear, and I'm not surprised. She's not all that keen on her husband right now, and Kyle has never gotten over her. Not that I approve of it, but the news doesn't come as a shock."

Kyle and Karla dated off and on throughout high school. She broke up with him right after their joint graduation party and moved to Kansas City the next week. Within months, she was married. Kyle played the field for years and then suddenly got engaged to a nineteen-year-old. However, she broke it off a few weeks before the wedding.

"You going to try to solve this murder, too?" Donna asked me.

"We'll see." I took a long drink of my beer, closed my eyes, and swayed back and forth while I sang along to "Benny and the Jets."

Aunt Star plucked the bottle from my hand and set it on the

bar. "Let's go, Elton. You've got to be at church in eight hours, and we don't need you falling asleep during the sermon."

Marty helped me off the stool, Donna gave me a hug, and Aunt Star steered me through the crowd without letting anyone stop us. We exited into the humid night air, and I took a few deep breaths to try to clear the smoke out of my lungs.

"I don't know how Donna can smoke those things," I said. "So disgusting."

"And bad for your health. But also extremely addicting." Aunt Star had smoked for a short time when she was in high school. But Mom had told her she couldn't be around me and my brother if she smoked, so she stopped, though it took a while for her to fully break the habit.

"Did you find it interesting that Donna and Marty were chatting by themselves instead of with a bigger group?" I asked over my shoulder as I stepped out into the street.

"Watch out!" Aunt Star grabbed my arm and pulled me back.

EIGHT

A BLACK PICKUP CAME to a stop several yards beyond us and then reversed back toward us. The tinted window rolled down to reveal Mitchell with a concerned look on his face.

"Hey there, handsome!" I chirped.

His eyes opened wide, and he tried to suppress a grin before shooting a questioning look at Aunt Star.

She said, "Your lovely date has consumed two beers in less than an hour, which is two more than normal. She's not quite herself at the moment."

"I see." He returned his gaze to me. "Be careful, okay? Maybe consider looking both ways before you cross the street?"

"Yes, sir!" I gave him a mock salute.

He sighed and gave Aunt Star an exasperated look.

"We're on our way home." She held her keys up and jangled them. "I'm driving."

He nodded.

"What are you doing?" I gave him a hopeful look. "Have you solved the murder?"

Mitchell laughed. "Not quite yet. Have you?"

"Nope. But I'm ...," I caught myself and then made finger guns at him, "... *not* trying." I gave him my biggest grin.

He raised his eyebrows. "Glad to hear it."

"Seriously, though," Aunt Star said to him, "what's up? You heading back to The Osh for the night?" The hotel was around the corner.

"I'm on my way there to check in and change into more comfortable clothes. Then I'll go back to the station for a few more hours." He waved his arm at all the vehicles up and down the street. "What's going on here? I've never seen this many cars parked on Main Street—even during the day."

"My classmates decided to move the reunion to The Blue Barn. They're packed in like sardines." I pressed my hands together to give him a visual.

Aunt Star pointed her thumb at me. "This one has to be at church in the morning, though, so I'm going to go put her in bed."

Music briefly burst from the bar's doorway as someone exited, and Mitchell shifted his car back into gear. "Keep her safe," he instructed my aunt. "Sweet dreams." He gave me a smile.

"You, too." I blew him an air kiss.

He chuckled and shook his head at me as he drove off.

Aunt Star took me by the elbow and steered me across the street and down the sidewalk. When she stopped to let a car go through the stoplight, I squinted at the pickup parked near us on the street. "Wait a minute. Didn't we already see that truck? Am I drunker than I thought?"

"No, that's Randy's pickup. We've only seen it once. Here we go. Time to cross the street."

———

THE CHURCH CHOIR DIRECTOR accosted me as soon as I entered the church door, which was not surprising, as she had done the same thing the morning after Aidan's murder. Suzanne peppered me with questions, and I held a hand up. "I'm not going to talk about the murder. I have stuff to do, and I think you do, too." Several months earlier, I would never have dreamed of talking to her in such a way, but our dynamic changed after she'd been accused of murder and I'd put myself in danger to help clear her name.

"Fine."

I was surprised she gave in so quickly, but I didn't question it. Instead of heading to the church office, where I knew she'd follow me in, I stepped into the first Sunday school room we came to and asked the teacher, Maggie, if she needed anything. She seemed puzzled, as she was always fully prepared, but when she spotted Suzanne hovering beyond me, understanding dawned in her eyes.

"Yes, I was wondering if you could give me any ideas for this craft I'm going to do with the kids," Maggie said.

I wasn't crafty in the least, and she knew it, and Suzanne knew it, but I confidently said, "I'd love to help."

Maggie ushered me further into the room and shut the door in Suzanne's face. I let out a sigh of relief.

"Thanks."

"You're welcome. I was being self-serving, too. I didn't want her asking me any questions either."

"Oh, yeah. You're Paula's cousin." I pulled her into a hug. "I'm so sorry."

She squeezed me tightly before letting go and sitting on one of the child-sized tables. "Thanks. But you probably knew her better than I did, being in her class and all."

She patted the table next to her and I sat.

"Until the reunion, I hadn't seen or talked to her since high school," I said. "Did you see much of her?"

"Only at big family gatherings—maybe once or twice a year?" She shrugged. "But you know how those things go. You get to really talk to only a handful of people, so I was rarely able to catch up with her. Most of what I know about her is from my mom."

Maggie's mom and Paula's mom were sisters. Maggie was five or six years ahead of us in school, so she and Paula were too far apart in age to be very close as kids.

I wanted to ask if her mom had recently told her anything about Paula that might give me a clue about who would have a motive to kill her, but I didn't know how to do it without being rude and doing exactly what I hadn't wanted Suzanne to do to me.

Before I could make up my mind if it was worth asking, she offered, "All I know is things had been a bit rough at their house since Zachary was born."

I didn't have time to respond to that revelation before the door burst open and two small children raced in. Maggie and I both greeted them, and then I slipped out the door after checking the hallway for Suzanne.

The choir members were warming up for practice when I walked past the choir room, which told me Suzanne would be occupied for the rest of the morning.

A different style of music was pumping out of the youth room as I approached it. When I entered the room, Greg was playing ping-pong with a few kids at the table in the corner, a boy and girl were sitting rather too close to each other on the couch in the opposite corner, and a handful of girls were singing along to the Petra song blaring from the boombox.

Greg spotted me and handed his paddle off to one of the kids watching the game. He started to head my way but made a quick detour to separate the kids on the couch. I hadn't noticed the two together before, so I made a mental note to keep an eye on the budding relationship. Not much affected the atmosphere of a youth group more negatively than a break-up between two members.

In the meantime, a pair of junior high girls entered and flanked me.

"Beckett!" One of them threw her arms around me. "We heard what happened at your reunion. That's *totally* awful. How can you even *deal* with it?" I could hear the italics in her voice, they were so pronounced.

I gently peeled her off me and assured her I was okay.

The other girl, Tiffani, sat on a nearby table and patted it in much the way Maggie had a few minutes earlier. "Come tell us everything." There was no way I was telling her anything. She couldn't keep her mouth shut, *and* she was Anita's niece. Though I did wonder if I could discover any information about Anita from her.

"Sorry, ladies," I said as Greg approached. "I can't really talk about it. I don't want to say anything that might put the investigation at risk."

"Ooh, yes, the investigation," Tiffani squealed. "Aunt Anita said your boyfriend is in charge." She wiggled her eyebrows at me.

Greg stiffened at that proclamation.

I cleared my throat. "Detective Crowe is not my boyfriend. He was just my date for the reunion."

"Just your *date,* huh?" the other girl said. "Yeah, sure."

The two of them giggled, and I did my best not to roll my eyes at them.

"All right, girls," Greg said, "why don't you go check in on the ping-pong game?"

The two girls scampered off, Greg pulled out a chair for me, and we both sat.

"I heard you tell them you're okay, but are you really?" he asked.

Thanks to my two beers the night before, I had dropped right off to sleep when we returned from The Blue Barn, so I was feeling fairly fresh, though Paula's death weighed on me. I also had a slight pit in my stomach due to the knowledge that one of my classmates was a murderer. And I had arrived at church fifteen minutes later than I was supposed to. But other than all that, I was doing just fine.

Greg didn't need all those details, though. "Not totally okay, but as well as you could expect. I hate to say it, but I already feel like I'm getting used to dealing with murders." I smoothed the skirt of my flower-print dress over my knees. "That's not something I want to get used to." Tears threatened to spill over, and I rolled my eyes toward the ceiling to try to keep them contained.

Greg reached his hand out like he was going to touch me, but then he pulled it back.

"No, I wouldn't want you to, either." He ran his fingers through his hair. He wore it in a mullet and was so self-conscious of it that I was surprised he hadn't cut it off.

A brother and sister entered the room. The boy headed off to the ping-pong table, but the girl held back near the door. The family was new to town, and Courtney was extremely shy. She had yet to fall into a comfortable friendship with any other girls in the youth group. I waved her over to the table.

"Hi, Miss Beckett. Hi, Pastor ... uh, Greg," Courtney said in a slight Southern accent.

I stopped myself from once again telling her to simply call us Beckett and Greg. The siblings' parents demanded they use formal names for adults, though none of the other church kids did. It had taken some convincing to get Courtney to at least use our first names instead of our last ones.

"I'm sorry to hear about your friend," she said to me.

I was surprised she knew about the murder and especially that I knew the deceased, since her family was so new to town.

"Thank you. I appreciate that." I smiled at her, and she gave me a tentative smile back.

Greg checked the time, stood, and clapped his hands twice.

"All right, kids, let's get this party started!"

The kids began to gather at the tables, and I made sure Courtney was sitting with Tiffani and her friend before heading out of the room and rushing down the hall to the office to check that Pastor Coker didn't need anything before I headed to my own Sunday school class.

————

WHEN I ENTERED THE sanctuary for the church service, I was slightly surprised to see Paula's mom Georgia sitting in her typical spot near the back of the room. Most people wouldn't have shown up to church the morning after their child was killed, but I couldn't recall Georgia ever missing church for anything. Veronica sat with her instead of in her "pastor's wife spot" along the center aisle in the front row. I wondered if Pastor Coker would mention anything about Paula from the pulpit.

Since my parents were out of town, I wasn't sure where to sit. I didn't want to sit alone in our usual pew on the third row, so I hesitated at the back of the room.

A hand grasped my arm. "Sit here with us," Tiffani said. She dropped my arm and motioned for the other teenagers in the back row to scoot down and make room for me.

I couldn't say no with all of them staring at me, so I took a seat.

"You really can't tell me anything about yesterday?" Tiffani asked.

"No." I kept looking straight ahead.

"How about if I tell *you* something?"

I whipped my head toward her. "What?"

She leaned over close to my ear. "Aunt Anita told me Paula and Billy didn't really get along. She's been to their house a few times and said it was chill-*ly,* and I'm not talking about the temperature, if you know what I mean." She nodded a few times to emphasize her point.

That was the second mention of potential marriage problems between the two. I wondered what the real issue was.

"She also said she thought they slept in different bedrooms."

I narrowed my eyes. "How would she know that?"

Tiffani shrugged.

NINE

BEFORE I COULD ASK Tiffani another question, Suzanne started the service with a rousing praise chorus from the choir, followed by two of my favorite hymns: "Bringing in the Sheaves" and "When the Morning Comes."

Pastor Coker stepped up onto the stage for his usual prayer time, but instead of launching right in, he cleared his throat, gripped the sides of the pulpit, and looked straight at Georgia before addressing the congregation.

"I'm thankful to see our dear sister Georgia here this morning. As you all likely know," his eyes swept the room, "her daughter Paula, a former member here at First Comm, passed away unexpectedly last night. Let's all keep Georgia and the rest of the family in our prayers."

As the pastor prayed, my thoughts wandered to Anita. Why would she tell her thirteen-year-old niece that Paula and Billy were having marriage issues? And when did she tell her—before or after Paula died?

This wasn't the time to think about that. I took a deep breath and focused on Pastor Coker's prayer. He asked for guidance for the police officers, which led my mind to wander again, but this time to Mitchell. I smiled but then quickly stifled it. The teens next to me likely didn't have their eyes closed, and I didn't want them to gossip about Mitchell and me any more than they already were.

The pastor said, "Amen," and the ushers passed the offering

plates while a choir member sang an Amy Grant song. As I sang along in my head, I scanned the bulletin and noticed a typo. I sighed. No doubt I'd hear about it from at least one church member.

The sermon title also caught my eye. Though I'd typed it, I hadn't paid much attention to it at the time, but it was a timely message: "Finding Hope in Suffering." As Pastor Coker began to preach, I hoped the teenagers' whispering wouldn't distract me too much.

———

AFTER CHURCH, NOBODY WAS talking about the murder, out of respect for Georgia. Nobody asked me any questions, and I didn't have the heart to try to find out any information either.

I typically ate lunch across the street at The Check with my parents after church, but since they were out of town, and Mitchell was occupied, I was at a loose end. The only other restaurant open on Sundays was the Dairy Queen, and I had decided to grab something at the DQ drive-through when I heard my name hissed down the church hallway. I turned to see Veronica hurrying toward me, pulling Georgia along with her.

She reached me and spoke so quietly I could barely hear her. "I've invited Georgia over to the house for lunch. I know your parents are out of town, so would you like to join us?" Her eyes darted back and forth down the hallway.

"Um, sure." I wondered why she was acting so strangely, but I wasn't about to ask.

"Meet us over there, but wait a few minutes."

"Ooookay."

"I'll explain later."

"Gotcha."

Veronica looked both ways again and scurried down the

hallway with Georgia.

I shook my head at her antics and continued to the office with the remaining stack of bulletins from the foyer. The office door was open, and Greg was on his hands and knees in front of a bookshelf.

"Looking for something in particular?"

He turned his head toward me but stayed on the floor. "Yes, there's a book somewhere here that I need for youth group on Wednesday." He resumed scanning the shelf. "Ah, here it is."

I set the bulletins on my desk as he stood with his book in hand.

"Why are you keeping those?" He motioned toward the stack.

"I always do. There are giant piles of them in the closet down the hall. As for why, I don't know. Pastor Coker told me to do it. I guess that's the way it's always been." I cocked my head to the side. "I should ask, though. Seems silly to have them taking up space down there."

Greg shifted the book from hand to hand and bit his lip

"What?" I swiped a hand across my mouth. "Is something on my lips?"

"Uh, no. I ... since your parents are out of town, I was wondering if you have lunch plans. Would you like to go to The Check with me?" He shifted on his feet. "I mean, I know you have your, uh ... detective guy, but I'm guessing he's busy. And this wouldn't be a date," he reassured me. "It's just ... I don't want you to have to eat alone. But then you do have your aunt, don't you?"

I cut in to put him out of his awkward misery. "I appreciate the thought, Greg, but I do have plans." I didn't want to tell him it was with the Cokers, since he might wonder why he wasn't invited too.

"Oh." He practically lunged toward the doorway. "I'll see you later then."

"Bye!" I shouted at his retreating back.

I straightened a few stacks of paper on my desk and then locked up and headed out. I crossed the nearly empty parking lot and rang the Cokers' doorbell. Within seconds the door jerked open. Veronica took me by the arm, pulled me inside, peeked outside, and then slammed the door.

"I thought I told you to wait."

"I did!" I insisted.

She huffed and led me toward the kitchen. The smell of roast beef had assaulted me the second the front door opened, so there was no question about the lunch menu.

Georgia was seated at the speckled, Formica-topped kitchen table. She gave me a wan smile, and I leaned over to give her a hug.

"What can I help with?" I asked Veronica, who was checking on the roast.

"Can you make some iced tea?" She pointed at a cabinet. "There's a jar of instant in there."

I pulled out the glass jar with a grimace and stood on my tiptoes to grab a Tupperware pitcher off the top of the fridge.

"Sweet?" I asked.

"Yes, please."

At least she got that part right.

I poured glasses of tea and joined Georgia at the table.

"The roast will take another fifteen minutes, and likely Harold will, too." Veronica took a seat. "Let's get down to business."

"What business?" I asked.

"The business of figuring out who killed Paula."

Georgia gasped, and I sat back in my chair.

"We're going to *what?*" Georgia asked in a shaky voice.

"Find out who murdered her. We've done it before." She waved her hand between herself and me. "And we can do it again."

Ding-dong!

Veronica jumped up to answer the door.

"Is she serious?" Georgia asked me.

"Pretty sure she is."

I heard my aunt's voice before I saw her.

"What are you doing here?" I inquired.

Veronica answered for Aunt Star. "I called her as soon as we got home and asked her to join us, too. I figured the two of you were already working on the case."

She directed Aunt Star to the seat beside me. I hadn't even noticed the table was set for five.

I got up to pour Aunt Star a glass of tea.

"As I was saying," Veronica said, "we're going to find out who killed Paula if it's the last thing we do." Her face turned red when she realized what she said.

"Don't worry about it." Georgia flapped her hand. "We don't realize how many of the flippant phrases we use are related to death until someone dies. I learned that when Bernard passed away."

"Before we go any further with this line of conversation," I looked at Georgia, "when is Tommy's family coming in?" Paula's brother Tommy was a preacher in Bentonville, Arkansas.

"They'll drive up late tonight after church. He's going to do the funeral. I told him he didn't have to, but he insisted." Tears filled her eyes.

"Do you know when you'll be able to have the funeral?"

"Not yet." She took a gulp of her iced tea. "They have to do an autopsy and I don't know what else. They said that might be done tomorrow, but they don't know for sure, what with the holiday coming up and all." She sniffled.

For her sake, I hoped it would be sooner rather than later. That would be better for the investigation, too. Speaking of investigations, I wasn't going to let Veronica take charge of our under-the-radar version.

I leaned toward Georgia and pushed my hand palm-up across the table toward her. She grasped it tightly.

"I know this is hard, Georgia. Not only have you lost your daughter, but you don't know why. Can you help us try to figure that out?"

She looked at each of us in turn, let go of my hand, and sat up straight. "I know you figured out who killed Aidan. But I also know you put yourself at risk to do so. I can't ask you to do that again."

"You're not asking. We're telling you we'll do it," Veronica said.

Aunt Star added, "And we'll do it whether you help us or not. But your help might make it happen more quickly." She looked at me. "Trixie's in, too. She called while you were at church, and I told her everything we learned last night. I hope that was okay."

"Yes."

Georgia shook her finger at us. "I'll help you, as long as you girls stick together and don't do anything stupid."

I smiled at her. "We'll do our best."

The back door opened, and Pastor Coker entered. He stopped short when he saw all of us at the kitchen table, and then he beamed.

"Ladies!" he boomed. "Excellent to see you all. Welcome, welcome."

"Yes, they know they're welcome. They've been here a while," Veronica said. "Now go wash up, and I'll get the food on the table."

He trundled down the hallway, and once the bathroom door shut, Veronica said in a stage whisper, "No more of this talk with him here. We can talk after lunch when he's taking his nap."

"Let's do it at our house," I suggested. "That way he won't

accidentally hear anything, and I'll see if Trixie can join us." And I could hopefully take and keep the upper hand in this investigation. After all, I was the one who cracked the case the last time.

"Wait. You're not telling your husband?" Georgia's forehead wrinkled.

"Heavens, no." Veronica huffed. "He'd have a stroke. But what he doesn't know won't hurt him."

"I guess that's all right." Georgia's voice betrayed her concern.

"Of course it is. I'm my own woman," Veronica remarked.

Nobody could argue with that.

———

"I HEREBY OPEN THE first official meeting of the Justice for Paula Club." I pounded my fist on our kitchen table like a gavel, making the glass panels rattle. "Whoops." I gave Aunt Star a sheepish look.

We had regathered at our house, and Trixie had joined us.

"First off, you do know she was poisoned, right?" I asked Georgia. I was careful not to mention the cyanide.

"Yes, the police mentioned that when they talked to me last night," Georgia said.

"Can you think of anyone who might have reason to hurt Paula?" I asked her. "Take your time." I picked up my pen and prepared to take notes in a small, spiral-bound notebook.

"I ... I really don't know. I can't imagine my girl would have done anything to deserve this." Her eyes filled with tears.

I handed her a box of tissues. "Most people don't deserve it. Well, maybe nobody deserves it. But I can guarantee Paula didn't. People kill for all kinds of reasons, and many of them don't make sense to the rest of society."

"Think about Aidan," Veronica said. "He didn't deserve to

die. The reasons seemed small and even silly to us. It's probably the same with Paula." She picked a chocolate chip cookie from the plate on the table and took a nibble.

"How about if we ask Georgia specific questions?" Trixie offered.

"Yes, that might work best." I thought for a moment. "This first one is a hard one, but it's going to be best if you're honest. Were Paula and Billy having any marriage problems?"

"Oh!" She looked horrified. "Do you think Billy could have done this?"

I couldn't imagine she hadn't thought of it, but not everybody knows the spouse is usually the prime suspect in a murder. And nobody wants to suspect their own son-in-law.

"I don't think so." Though I couldn't completely discount him, much as it pained me. "But we need to cover all our bases."

"Okay. Well, everything was just fine between them for the longest time. I mean, they had their squabbles, like everyone does, but nothing major. But after Zachary was born ..." Her eyes turned glassy, and her gaze focused somewhere over my left shoulder.

"Yes?" Aunt Star said. "What happened after Zachary was born?"

Georgia shook her head to refocus. "I don't know if all of you know this, but it was a difficult birth."

Everyone nodded but me. I guessed I didn't know about it because I wasn't living Cherry Hill at the time. I was in St. Louis, but I hadn't kept in touch with the couple after high school, even though we lived in the same city.

"Both Paula and Zachary were in the hospital for a few weeks, and once they got home, Paula wouldn't let him out of her sight. She wouldn't get a babysitter so she and Billy could go to a movie or business dinners or anything. She wouldn't spend time with friends. I was surprised when she said she was going to that wedding yesterday. They let her take Zachary with her, or she wouldn't have. It was also a miracle she went to the reunion, since kids weren't invited."

Georgia twisted a napkin in her hands. "They occasionally hosted people for dinner, but only at Billy's invitation. Paula was always upset when he did it. I tried to encourage her to spend more time with Billy and with other women, but I don't think she did. She has been completely focused on Zachary for the past three years." A tear ran down her cheek. "Had been."

Veronica reached over and took Georgia's hand.

Georgia continued, "Billy started spending a lot more time at the office. He'd come home late—often after Zachary was already in bed, and sometimes even Paula. He started sleeping in the guest room most of the time. And they fought—a lot." She held her hand up. "Not physical fighting. He never laid a hand on her, as far as I knew."

I didn't think any of that would be reason enough for Billy to kill Paula. He might want to divorce her, but poisoning seemed farfetched.

"Do you know what they fought about Friday night?" I asked Georgia.

She gave me a sharp look. "How do you know they had a fight?"

"Billy told me. That's why he came down early. Paula told him not to go to the wedding with her."

"Oh. I didn't know about any of that. They were staying with the Arbuckles last night, so I didn't see any of them yesterday."

Georgia broke down in sobs, and Veronica scooted her chair right next to Georgia's so she could put an arm around her. The rest of us made small talk while she composed herself.

She wiped her eyes and took a deep breath. "Sorry about that. Let's keep going."

"No need to apologize," I said. "Did Paula ever mention Anita Nichols visiting them?"

TEN

ANGER FLICKERED IN GEORGIA'S eyes at the mention of Anita's name. "Yes. Billy invited her over for dinner a few times. Paula thought they might be having an affair, but I told her if that were the case, he wouldn't invite Anita over to the house. Paula said Anita did shamelessly flirt with Billy, though, right in front of her and Zachary. The hussy." Georgia's eyes widened and she clapped her hand over her mouth. "I shouldn't have said that."

She lowered her hand and said, "I know all of this sounds bad for Billy. But he's not a violent man." She gave me a piercing look. "You should know that."

I nodded, and Veronica gave me a speculative look, but she didn't ask what Georgia was talking about. I figured she would interrogate me later.

Veronica did ask, "What about this Anita person? Who is she? Sounds like she might have wanted Paula out of the way."

I ate two cookies while Trixie explained who Anita was and how she had changed since high school.

I wiped the crumbs from my mouth. "And she's indiscreet enough to talk about Paula and Billy's marriage in front of her niece, Tiffani." I told them what Tiffani said at church, which lined up with what Georgia told us.

"Ah, Anita is Tiffani's aunt," Veronica said.

"Yes, her mom's sister." Tiffani's dad's family had always gone to First Comm, but Anita's family didn't attend church.

I turned to the front page of my notebook, where I had written

"SUSPECTS" at the top. I wrote Billy and Anita's names under it.

Georgia cleared her throat when she saw Billy's name.

"Sorry, Georgia, but even though I don't think he did it, we can't fully discount him."

"Who else can we add?" Aunt Star asked.

"Karla," Trixie said.

"Karla James?" Georgia looked confused. "Why would she have anything against Paula?"

I told her about Karla and her husband losing a lot of money on an investment.

"But that's not Billy's fault!" Georgia objected.

"No, but Karla seems to think it is. That's a decent motive." I added her name to the list.

"Why would she take it out on Paula instead of Billy, though?" Georgia shook her head.

"Maybe she thought since he took something valuable from her, she would take something valuable from him," Aunt Star said.

I tapped my notebook with my pen. "On a semi-related topic, does anybody know if something is going on between Marty James and Donna Jenkins? They were noticeably comfortable with each other last night at The Blue Barn. I've never seen them together before."

"Not that I know of," Trixie said. "She's never said anything about him at school."

"I hadn't seen them together before last night," Aunt Star said.

Georgia added, "I've *never* seen them together."

"Donna could have simply been trying to stay away from Jeff," Trixie guessed.

"What happened between those two?" Donna and Jeff had split up before I moved back to Cherry Hill, though their divorce had only recently been finalized.

"She's been vague about that," Trixie said. "And you know me. I'm not going to pry. The divorce was nasty, though."

"I guess it's good they didn't have any kids," Aunt Star commented.

"Okay, back to our suspects." I picked up my pen again. "Is there anyone else we can think of?" I focused on the woman across from me. "Georgia?"

"I can't think of anything else. I don't know that she kept in touch with anyone else in your class."

"Donna said Cheryl talked to Paula sometimes," I offered.

"Paula hasn't—hadn't—mentioned anything about Cheryl for a while," Georgia said, "or Donna. She and Jeff used to visit with Paula and Billy when they were in the city. But that would have stopped after Zachary was born."

"Speaking of Donna," Trixie said, "she's a science teacher."

We all stared at her for a moment until I caught on to what she was saying.

"So she might know more about poisons than the average person," I said.

"Makes sense," Veronica said.

"But what would her motive be?" Aunt Star asked. "It sounds like she hadn't been in contact with Paula for a while. Plus, she's the one who called and invited you to The Blue Barn last night. Would the murderer do that?"

"Seems unlikely," I said, "but I'll add her to the list."

"Do we know for sure it was someone at the reunion?" Veronica asked.

"It almost certainly was," I explained about the locked back door and not seeing anyone who shouldn't have been there. "It could have been two people working together, but that's doubtful."

Brrrring!

Aunt Star stood and answered the phone. I could tell it was

Darren by the tone of her voice when she discovered who was calling.

"Okay," she said, "I'll tell her. ... Bye."

She hung up the phone and focused her gaze on me while retaking her seat.

"They want you to come down to the station to answer a few more questions."

"What questions?"

She shrugged. "Beats me."

"Are we done here?" I looked at everyone in turn.

Nobody spoke up, so I flipped my notebook shut.

———

WHEN I ENTERED THE police station, I was surprised someone other than Barbara Young was seated at the desk in the reception area. Then I remembered it was Sunday, and Barbara worked weekdays. I didn't recognize the woman at the desk.

"Can I help you?" she asked.

"Yes, Darren ... I mean Deputy Chief Turley asked me to come in. I'm Beckett Monahan."

Before she could respond, Frank appeared in the doorway beyond the desk. "Becky, come on back."

Frank escorted me through "the pit," an open area filled with officers' desks, and toward an interview room. Darren was on the phone in his office at the back of the room, and he spotted me through his window. He pointed to the phone, and I waved at him. Mitchell wasn't in the chief's office, and I wondered where he was.

I settled into one of the sturdy wooden chairs at the table in the interview room, and Frank brought me a can of Diet Coke.

"Deputy Chief Turley should be off the phone in a minute, and Detective Crowe will be here soon."

"Oh?" I said nonchalantly. "Where has he been?"

He shook his head at me from the doorway. "Becky, you know I'm not supposed to tell you anything."

"Yeah, not about the investigation. But I'm asking about my *friend*, Mitchell." I beamed at him.

He chuckled. "You're not going to get me, young lady, so stop trying."

I tried a different tactic. "I enjoyed catching up with Anita yesterday."

"I haven't talked to the girl yet since she's been in town. Been a little busy. She'll be here all week, though, her mama said."

"I didn't know she moved to St. Louis until she mentioned it last night." I propped my chin on my hand and looked at Frank like I expected a response.

"Yep. Moved there around Christmas time." He left the doorway and sat across from me. "Didn't really give a reason. Said she needed a change."

"Is she still an accountant?" I cracked my soda can open and took a drink.

"No. She's doing something different with stocks or investing or something. Like what Billy Arbuckle does, I think."

"A financial advisor?" I took another sip.

He slapped the table, and my head jerked in response, resulting in a few drops of Diet Coke dribbling onto my dress. I tried to pat them dry with my hand.

"Yep, that's it."

How had that not come to light yet? Maybe Anita and Billy had spent more time together than anyone knew.

Mitchell appeared in the doorway. I sucked in a breath at the view of his muscular form in tapered black pants and a fitted white button-up shirt and tie. He leaned against the doorjamb and loosened his tie. He held my gaze as he slowly removed the tie and unbuttoned the top few buttons of his shirt. My blush and lack of attention alerted Frank to Mitchell's presence, and he jumped to his feet.

"Here you go, Detective Crowe." Frank waved toward his vacated chair. "See you later, Becky."

Mitchell draped the tie over the back of the chair, took a seat, propped his elbows on the table, and gave me a lazy smile. "What are you doing here? Not that I'm sorry to see you."

"You don't know why I'm here? Darren called and asked me to come in to answer some questions."

"I've been out. Darren's on the phone, but he pointed me this way."

His gaze traveled down from my face. "You're awfully dressed up for a police interview."

"Haven't had time to change since church."

He glanced at his watch and raised his eyebrows at me. He had reason to be curious, since it was past three o'clock and my original plan was to spend the entire afternoon with him. I wasn't about to tell him exactly what I'd been up to, though.

"My pastor's wife invited me over for lunch. They're quite the talkers," was all the explanation I gave.

"How did Darren find you if you were over there?" Nothing got past him.

"Um, I was home by then." I shifted uncomfortably in my seat.

Darren kept Mitchell from continuing his line of questioning by striding through the door and closing it behind him. He sat next to Mitchell, flipped open his notebook, and hit "record" on the tape player on the table next to me. He stated the date and everyone's names.

"Wow. I didn't realize this was so serious. What's going on?" I glanced between the two men, though I knew Mitchell had no clue either.

Darren took a deep breath. "Why didn't you tell us you dated Billy in high school?"

I folded my arms in front of my chest, and Mitchell gave me a sharp look.

"It didn't occur to me to mention it. And everybody in our class knew, so I guess I didn't think to tell you. How is that relevant?"

"It's relevant because I hear it wasn't a friendly break-up."

"You're right. It wasn't. But I got over it a long time ago—even before high school was over."

"Care to tell us what happened?"

Mitchell slowly opened his own notebook and focused on it instead of me.

"Billy was my first boyfriend. We started dating at the end of our freshman year. We had our bad moments, as everyone does, but mostly things were good. I thought we'd get married."

I shot a glance at Mitchell, who was still focused on his notebook.

"Then during the summer before our senior year, I was gone to church camp for a week. Normally, Paula would have been there too, but she was lifeguarding at the pool that summer, and she couldn't get a full week off work. I was home from camp less than an hour when I got a call from Karla James." For Mitchell's sake, I said, "Now Karla Bright."

He finally looked up and gave me an almost imperceptible nod. His expression was blank.

"We were never friends, so I knew something was up the moment I heard her voice. She couldn't wait to tell me Billy spent all day every day at the pool that week and used much of that time to flirt with Paula, buy her snacks, and basically make a fool of himself. She said everybody was talking about it."

"You must have been angry," Darren suggested.

I narrowed my eyes at his leading statement. "I was both angry and mortified. I should have waited a while to calm down, but I was seventeen, so of course I didn't. I marched straight over to his house and confronted him. He tried to deny it, but I didn't believe him. Say what you will about Karla, but she's a straight shooter. I also knew she'd have no reason to lie about something plenty of other people could back up.

"I stormed off and refused to talk to Billy when he tried to call later that night. The next day he came over to the house and finally admitted it. He promised he still loved me, and he thought we could go back to the way things were. He was wrong." I shrugged. "Not only did he betray me, but he also lied about it, and he didn't apologize. Paula and I were close friends until then. Not as close as I was with Trixie, but since we both attended First Comm, we spent a lot of time together."

A knock sounded on the door, and Frank popped his head in.

"Boss, there's a call for you. You're going to want to take it."

Darren gave me an assessing look. "I'll be right back. Don't go anywhere."

He hit pause on the tape player and stood. He purposefully pushed the door all the way open on his way out.

"Why didn't you tell me your ex-boyfriend would be at the reunion? You could have given me some warning," Mitchell said quietly.

"I honestly didn't think about it. It was so long ago. It doesn't matter anymore."

"Some people would say it's motive."

"Do *you* say it's motive?"

"In theory, yes. Knowing it's you, no. But we can't simply let it go, specifically because it's you."

I sighed. "I get that."

We gazed at each other in silence for a while before my neck started to heat.

I swept my hand toward his torso. "So did you run home to get more clothes, or what?"

He looked down. "This is what I brought to wear to church

today. I'll need to go pick up some more clothes at some point, though."

"You were going to go to church with me?"

I hadn't asked him to do so, partly because he would have needed to arrive separately from me since I had to get there so early, and partly because I wanted to avoid questions from curious church members if he made an appearance.

"Of course." He reached across the table and covered my hand with his, sending tingles all the way to my toes. "I wanted to spend as much time with you as I could."

Darren cleared his throat loudly as he re-entered and shut the door, and we slid our hands apart. I wondered how much he had heard.

He hit the pause button again and stated the time. "Let's finish your story. Only the pertinent details, please."

I was taken aback by his terseness, but he had a lot on his plate, so I didn't comment on it. "I broke up with Billy. He was livid."

"How did he show his anger?" Darren asked.

"He didn't hit me, if that's what you're asking."

Mitchell got more specific. "Did he hit inanimate objects? Did he throw things?"

"No. He's not like that. He just yelled."

Darren's chair screeched as he scooted it back in an attempt to get more comfortable. I doubted he succeeded, because the chairs were decidedly hard and unyielding.

"Then what?" Darren asked.

"For one, I avoided the pool for the rest of the summer."

Mitchell chuckled. "I bet you did."

I grinned at him. Darren cleared his throat again.

"Sorry. By the time school started, the two of them were dating. I tried to avoid them, but that's not possible at a small school in a small town, so I was forced to deal with it. By the time we graduated, we were all on speaking terms again. Trixie helped a lot. Scott was in Vietnam, so we spent a lot of time together that year."

"Scott's a vet?" Mitchell cut in.

"Army. He was drafted. He doesn't like to talk about it."

"I understand that." Mitchell had spent time in Vietnam as well.

"That's pretty common." Darren pursed his lips at me. "Go on."

"Anyway, I started dating someone else, which helped me get over Billy and realize he wasn't the only man in the world. I even realized he wasn't right for me. Full disclosure," I gave them both pointed looks but for different reasons, "the other guy I dated was Jeff Jenkins. It was nothing serious. I was very clear about that from the start. He wasn't the kind of guy I wanted to marry, but he was fun. When I moved to St. Louis after high school, Jeff and I broke up—amicably, for the record—and soon after that, he and Donna got together."

"Anything else you need to tell us about Billy?" Darren asked.

"I didn't hold any grudges against Billy or Paula, but I also didn't keep in touch with them after high school, even though we all lived in St. Louis. I moved on."

Darren shoved his notebook and pen into his shirt pocket. He stood but paused before turning toward the door. "One more question: Did anyone take pictures at the reunion before Paula was found?"

"Hmm. I never thought to get my camera out with all the hubbub, but let me think." I closed my eyes and pictured the scene at the reunion. "Yes! Cheryl was taking some. I remember, because she was using one of those fancy thirty-five-millimeter cameras."

"Great. Thanks."

Mitchell and I stood to leave.

"Who was on the phone?" I asked Darren.

"Good grief, Beckett. You know I'm not going to tell you."

"I had to try."

He ushered me out of the room and escorted me all the way to the front door. I had hoped for a few more minutes with Mitchell, but Darren wasn't in a generous mood. Instead, I made do with a wave and a smile.

ELEVEN

AUNT STAR WAS COOKING spaghetti when I arrived home. I headed straight to the stove, lifted the skillet lid, and took a long sniff of the bubbling marinara sauce.

"Go change into something more comfortable," Aunt Star said. "I'll put the noodles on and the garlic bread in the oven, so be back down in ten minutes."

I headed upstairs, pulled on a tank top and shorts, and pulled my hair into a ponytail with a neon pink and yellow scrunchie.

As I set the table, I told Aunt Star about my experience at the police station.

"I forgot to mention to Darren and Mitchell what Frank said about Anita becoming a financial advisor."

"I would think they know. And is it really that important? Having the same job as someone else doesn't necessarily mean anything."

I pulled out a serving bowl for the sauce and set it by the stove. "But what if she did it to get close to Billy?"

"That's going a bit far, don't you think? Changing your career and moving to a new city to be close to a married man?"

"You're right. I'm sure there's nothing to that. But even if that wasn't her reason for moving and switching jobs, once she did it, she could have capitalized on the fact that she was in the same line of work as Billy to try to spend time with him."

"Maybe. I don't think that's worth mentioning to Darren or Mitchell, though. And like I said, they probably already know."

I thought for a minute. "From what Georgia said, I can't see Anita as a real suspect, especially if her motive was to be with Billy. Based on everything we've heard, she was in a position to know there was a decent chance Billy and Paula might divorce. Why not wait for that to happen—or even try to hurry along the separation—instead of killing Paula?"

We got everything on the table, said grace, and dug in.

"I wonder if they'll find anything important in Cheryl's pictures," I said after I downed a few bites.

"Won't it take a few days to get them developed?"

"The newspaper has a darkroom, and there's one in the high school art room. I would guess they'll get somebody to develop the film in one of those places."

"Probably not the newspaper, because they won't want Edna to know what they find," Aunt Star said.

"True."

Edna Thorn was the editor of our weekly local newspaper, *The Cherry Hill Standard*. She was fair, but she was also justifiably nosy.

"But," I added, "if they do go to the newspaper, I might be able to convince Edna to tell me what they find. I could trade information or something."

"Beckett!"

"What? I wouldn't tell her anything too important—nothing that would impede the investigation if it ended up in the paper this week. I'm going to go by the *Standard* office in the morning and see what I can find out."

"And what if the police are there when you stop by?" She dipped her garlic bread into her spaghetti sauce and took a bite.

"I'll think of something."

She nodded as she chewed. "You're going to Jazzercise tomorrow, right? We don't have it on Thursday this week, since that's a holiday."

I added, "I'll be there, but I need to go straight to Suzanne's afterward to work on the parade float."

Suzanne LaHaye's house was near the starting point of the Fourth of July parade route, and she had a giant garage, so First Comm always created our float at her place. We'd done it there for as long as I could remember.

"I'll be working on the float the next two nights as well, unless we get done early. But that has never happened, in my experience. Suzanne always finds something we can improve on. Though maybe one of those evenings will be Paula's funeral visitation. No way to know yet."

"Don't forget lunch tomorrow at The Check with Veronica and Trixie."

Georgia wasn't going to continue meeting with us, which was understandable. But she told us she'd let Veronica know if she thought of anything else that might be important.

"I'm hoping Callie can give us some info," Aunt Star said.

My aunt's lifelong best friend Callie Collister was a waitress at The Check. She was a fount of information even when you didn't necessarily need it.

"I'm also meeting Trixie at the library in the morning to find out everything we can about cyanide."

Aunt Star's forehead wrinkled. "Isn't cyanide what they found in medicine bottles a few years ago that killed a bunch of people?"

"Yes. Anyway, once I figure out how people can get their hands on it, that might help us figure out who might have the means."

"How are you going to do all of this investigating around town without Harold wondering what you're doing?"

Pastor Coker was usually in the office most of the day on Mondays, so that could pose a problem.

"I definitely can't lie to him." Not that I was in the habit of lying to anyone.

"Nope."

"Maybe I can tack my investigations on to other errands, like my bank run."

"The bank is across the street from the church. How long does it take you to make a deposit? Three minutes?"

"Okay, fine, that won't work."

I took my plate to the sink, grabbed a cookie from the strawberry-shaped cookie jar, and offered Aunt Star one. She declined, and she gave the cookie jar a dirty look. She hated the thing, but since I filled it with cookies—that she mostly ate when I wasn't around—she let me keep it out where everyone could see it.

"I could use the parade float as an excuse." I leaned back against the counter and nibbled the cookie. "I can go get some kind of supplies for it."

"That might do the trick." She started clearing the rest of the table. "You want to watch a movie? I rented *Against All Odds* yesterday. I had miraculously convinced Darren to watch it with me last night, but as you know, that didn't happen."

"Sure."

We loaded the dishwasher, and I took my usual spot on the couch while Aunt Star popped the video into the VCR. She hit "play," and the end credits were rolling. We both groaned on cue.

"Why can't people rewind?" I whined.

"Because they're not as kind as you are."

I WAS THE FIRST person in the office on Monday morning, which meant I could listen to the radio without anyone getting annoyed. I tuned in to Y107, and "Axel F" was playing. It blew my mind that an instrumental song was one of the top hits in the country, but *Beverly Hills Cop* had made it famous, and the tune was rather catchy.

Since I was alone, I felt comfortable pulling out my suspect notebook and perusing my notes. As I read back through them, I wondered if Billy truly was capable of murder. I couldn't see it, but so many times when you saw the friends, neighbors, and family members of murderers on the news, they would say, "He was such a normal guy. I never would have imagined he could do this." That's exactly what I would say about Billy.

However, Billy had a better way out of his strained marriage than murder: divorce. If he wanted Paula out of his life, a divorce wouldn't be easy, but it would have been doable. And he had Zachary to consider. Billy wouldn't kill his son's mother and put himself in the position of potentially going to prison for the rest of his life.

The door swung open, and I scrambled to close the notebook, but Greg noticed the movement. His eyes slightly narrowed. "What's that?"

"Um, nothing." I slowly slid the notebook under a pile of papers on my desk.

Greg's eyes followed my every move.

"Uh-huh."

He looked at the radio, which was now playing "Smooth Operator." "Mind if I change the station?"

"Go for it."

He turned the knob until he landed on a country station. I only listened to country music when I let Greg control the office radio or when I was with Trixie, but I'd heard enough of it lately to recognize "Girls' Night Out" by the Judds. They were Trixie's current favorite band.

Greg leaned back against his desk and crossed his arms. "If you're not going to tell me what you're up to," he nodded his head toward the covered notebook, "at least tell me how you're doing."

"Better than yesterday, but it's weird to think it happened," I admitted. "Paula and I were close when we were kids, but I hadn't kept in touch since we graduated. Now I wish I had."

I realized I truly meant that, especially after knowing what she'd been dealing with the past few years. Maybe I could have helped in some way. That was doubtful, but you never knew.

"That's understandable. You couldn't have known something like this would happen, though."

"No."

I looked at the clock on the wall across from my desk. I needed to meet Trixie at the library in ten minutes.

"Somewhere you need to be?" Greg asked.

Pastor Coker saved me from answering by barreling through the door. He gave me the same concerned look he had given me throughout lunch the day before. "You doing all right?"

"I'm fine." I glanced toward Greg. He raised his eyebrows but didn't say anything.

"Glad to hear it."

I said, "Since both of you are here, I'm going to go do my rounds of the classrooms and then run a few errands. I need to get some stuff for the float."

Pastor Coker nodded, and Greg said he'd answer the phone while I was gone. I shoved my notebook into my purse and scurried out into the hall before they could say anything else or I could betray my true motives.

I rushed through the Sunday school classrooms in record time, checking supply levels and making sure all was in order. Then I slipped out the back door of the church and hurried a few blocks down to the library. Trixie's brown Ford Bronco was in the parking lot.

I hesitated at the door when I spied Cheryl Stouffer at the check-out desk inside. I hadn't considered the fact that she was one of our town librarians when we made our research plan. I wanted to talk to her, but I also didn't want her to wonder why I was at the library instead of at work. Since there was nothing I could do about that now, and Krystal had already spotted me through the plate-glass window, I entered.

Trixie's daughter rushed over to hug me, and her brother Victor gave me a shy smile and wave from the children's section. I scanned the room for Trixie, but she was nowhere to be seen.

"Did you have fun with your grandma and grandpa on Saturday?" I asked Krystal.

"We did! They took us to the pool and to Dairy Queen and then we went to Home Video and got to pick out *any* movie we wanted to rent. Well, we had to agree," she pointed to Victor and then herself, "which was hard, but we picked *The Muppets Take Manhattan.* It was *so* funny!" She laughed at the memory.

"I'm glad you enjoyed yourselves," I said.

"Look what I'm reading!" She held her book right in front of my face. I leaned back to focus on the title.

"Ramona Quimby, Age 8," I read. "That's perfect, since you're eight!"

"I know! It's really good." She smiled and then skipped back to a beanbag chair in the children's section.

"Hey, Becky," Cheryl said in a monotone voice. I didn't have to wonder why she was not her usual chipper self.

"I wasn't sure you'd be here today," I said.

"I didn't really feel like it, but Kate is out of town. It was me or nobody."

"How *are* you feeling?"

Tears welled up in her eyes. "I'm sad and angry and still can't believe it's real. And I can't get the image of her out of my mind." She shook her head vigorously as if trying to shake the image away.

"I know exactly how that feels."

She looked at me sharply but then understanding dawned in her eyes. "Yes, you do. I'm sorry."

"Me, too."

"Does it get better?"

"It does, but it's something we'll both have to live with for the rest of our lives."

She nodded morosely.

"It might help if you think of some happy memories you have with Paula. What's your favorite memory of her?"

She perked up a bit at that, and she told me about a concert she and Randy went to with Paula and Billy before Zachary was born. Then her smile faded.

"Once Zachary came along, though, everything changed. I went to visit her in the hospital—you know they were both there for a few weeks—but after that, anytime I mentioned coming to visit, she'd put me off. She changed after that." Cheryl didn't elaborate, and I didn't push her, since Georgia had already filled us in on Paula.

"That's really hard." I kept myself from looking at my watch. I really needed to find Trixie, get my other sleuthing done, and get back to church, but I also didn't want Cheryl to feel like I was abandoning her.

"Yeah. Oh, Trixie asked me to tell you she's back in the non-fiction section. Not sure what she's looking for. She wouldn't let me help her."

"All right. You take care, Cheryl."

"I'll try."

Trixie was sitting on the floor between the shelves near the back of the library with books spread all around her.

"There's tables for that, you know."

"I do, but then I'd have to carry the books back and forth, and what's the point in that?"

"You're blocking the aisle."

She raised her eyebrows. "Do you see a crowd trying to get through?"

"No."

She tipped her head at me.

"Okay, fine." I dropped down next to her. "What have you learned?"

"Well, there's different types of cyanide."

She started explaining in detail, but I wasn't all that interested in the chemical makeup. "Yeah, yeah. Tell me in basic terms."

"There's one kind that's used in gas form, and there's one that's crystallized. That must be the one the killer used, or we'd all be dead." Trixie wasn't one to beat around the bush. "If the concentration of poison is high enough, a person can die within a few minutes. First, they feel nauseous and often dizzy or even giddy. Then they vomit and start breathing rapidly, followed by convulsions or muscle spasms, and then they die."

"That does sound like what happened to Paula. The blood Scott saw could be from hitting her head while convulsing." I shivered. "I wonder if she was dead or alive when I was in there. She obviously wasn't on the floor, but maybe she was kind of propped against the wall and hadn't fallen off yet. You know how narrow those stalls are."

"You said that so matter-of-factly," Trixie said. "I hate that you're getting used to talking about dead people."

"Hey!"

"I don't mean it like that. You're far from heartless. I'm saying I hate that death is now a common enough topic for us it's not a huge deal anymore."

"It's so weird."

Her eyes scanned the books on the shelf in front of her, and she pulled another one out.

I asked, "So where does somebody get cyanide—the crystal kind?"

"Lots of places. It's in some rat poisons and other pesticides. They use it for something with mining. And some photo developing solutions include cyanide." She turned to the index at the back of the book and ran her finger down the page.

"Hmm. So lots of people could have it or get their hands on it."

"Yes," she said, "especially farmers."

"Interesting. Too bad there are no farmers on our suspect list. And speaking of photo developing, I need to run over to the newspaper office and see if Edna knows anything."

"What are you talking about?"

"Oh yeah, the photo conversation happened after I left you." I filled her in.

"Go on, then. I'm going to keep at this to see if anything gives me an idea."

I held on to a nearby shelf to help steady myself as I stood from the floor, but it wobbled, and several books fell to the floor.

"Watch it!"

"Sorry." I grabbed the books and stuffed them back on the shelf.

Cheryl was talking to another library patron when I left, so I waved at Trixie's kids and headed back up the street to *The Cherry Hill Standard* office. A bell jingled on the door when I entered, and I approached the high counter in the front part of the building.

"We're all back here!" Edna Thorn hollered from somewhere further back. "Come on back, whoever you are!"

I stepped around the counter and past an unoccupied desk covered with handwritten notes and then passed through a small hallway into the large, high-ceilinged newsroom, where all the action happened. Of course, when the newspaper staff consists of four people, the action is probably never very lively, but the atmosphere seemed charged, and the air held the woody scent of newsprint.

"Beckett!" Edna was one of the rare few Cherry Hill residents who always got my name right on the first try. "What brings you to our humble newsroom?"

I wavered for a moment but then dove right into my true intentions. I didn't have time to beat around the bush.

"Did the police ask to use your darkroom last night?"

"Why, yes, they did. How did you know?"

I wanted to be vague, but then I realized that might make it seem like Mitchell was feeding me information, which wouldn't be helpful for either of us.

"I was at the police station yesterday answering some questions, and they asked me if anyone took pictures at the reunion. I knew they'd have to get the photos developed here or at the high school."

Edna peered at me over the top of her glasses. "If you ever need a job, come see me. You have an investigative mind."

"I'll hold you to that."

"Of course, we likely don't pay any better than the church does. Not much money in newspapers or religion." She pushed her glasses up her nose. "Anyway, yes, I developed the photos for them. I'm sure they would have preferred using the school, but they couldn't get ahold of anyone with access who knew how to use the darkroom. So they were stuck with me." She grinned. "Their loss is my gain."

And mine.

"Did you happen to look at the photos?"

She peered at me over her glasses again for a long moment, as if assessing me. Then she crooked a finger and headed toward a door near the back of the room. I followed her into a small office that was stuffed to the gills with books, newspapers, photos of Edna with local and regional celebrities, and random items like a ceramic kangaroo and a green basketball. Edna shut the door and plopped into the wooden rolling chair at her desk. She motioned me toward the other chair in the room, on which teetered a pile of newspapers. I moved the stack to the floor and took a seat.

"Now," she said, "I know you solved Aidan Patrick's murder, and I'm guessing you're trying to solve this one, too."

She waited for me to nod.

"That's why I'm helping you," she said. "But I need you to help me by keeping this between us. Got it?"

I couldn't agree. I needed to be able to tell the others what I learned.

"What's the problem?" she asked when I hesitated.

"I'm not the only one working on this. I've got a team helping me. I have to be able to tell my aunt Starla, Trixie Wallace, and Veronica Coker."

Her eyes narrowed when I said Veronica's name.

"I don't like that woman."

"She's not the easiest person to like, but she's a good person, and she knows how to keep a secret. *And* she helped catch Aidan's killer."

"Okay, but if I hear anyone else knows about this, my job offer is rescinded. And your subscription will be cancelled."

"I hear you."

She opened a desk drawer, pulled out a manila envelope, and handed it to me.

"I made doubles of all the photos. They cannot leave this office. But you can look at them now and even come back later if you need to." She stood. "Stay as long as you want."

TWELVE

EDNA SWEPT OUT OF the room, and I poured the photos out of the envelope onto my lap. A few fell to the floor, and I snatched them up before Edna could come back and see how I was treating her property.

I quickly flipped through all the pictures, and then I went back and inspected each one more closely. I scooted my chair up to Edna's desk, pulled out my notebook, and wrote down who was in each photo, especially when Paula was present.

In one of the last photos, Billy and Jeff Jenkins were talking in the foreground, and Paula was in the background. She was a little out of focus, but she was clearly holding a cup of punch and was in a group of people. A few of the others were obstructed by people closer to the camera, but Karla, Kyle, and Donna were all in view. Karla also held a cup, but I couldn't see Donna and Kyle's hands.

In the next photo, Karla and Kyle were no longer in the shot, and Donna and Paula were standing with one other person, but I couldn't tell who. All I could see was a woman's bare elbow. The back of Paula's hand was pressed to her forehead, as if she wasn't feeling well. I picked up the next snapshot, but it was of a completely different scene. Trixie and Anita were chatting by the door, so that shot would have been taken while I was in the bathroom.

I checked my watch and quickly scooped up the photos, put them back in the envelope, and shoved them into Edna's drawer.

Pastor Coker and Greg would not only be curious about my long absence but also worried. I rushed through the newsroom, thanked Edna as I passed, and walked back to the church as fast as my bad leg would allow.

The exertion left me breathing hard when I entered the office, which I realized too late would concern the men even more.

"Beckett! Where have you been? Are you okay?" Greg circled his desk, took me by the shoulders, leaned over to my eye level, and looked back and forth at my eyes.

Pastor Coker came out of his office. "Tell us what happened." His eyes darted around the office, as if he'd find a would-be assailant hiding behind a file cabinet.

"I'm fine. I got distracted." I had a split second to think of an excuse that wasn't a lie. "I ran into Cheryl Stouffer—you know, my classmate who found Paula."

Greg let his hands drop. "Oh, good. I mean, not good for her. But good that you're fine."

"How is Cheryl doing?" Pastor Coker asked.

"She's still pretty upset."

He nodded knowingly.

I scooted around my desk and dropped into my chair. Pastor Coker sat in one of the guest chairs near my desk.

"Many calls while I was gone?" I asked.

Greg sat on his desk. "A few. Mostly people wanting to know when and where the funeral will be. I hated to disappoint them, but we don't know yet."

"And Minnie Jensen called," Pastor Coker said.

"*Déjà vu,*" I said. Minnie had also called the church office the Monday morning after Aidan was killed. "What did she want?"

Minnie was both a busybody and an atheist who thrived on debating religion.

"She thought it was interesting that in the past few months we've had two murders connected to our church. Wondered if we were doing something wrong."

I came up out of my chair. "What?!"

"It's okay, dear," Pastor Coker said. "You know how she can be."

Greg and I both nodded. I settled myself back into my seat and took a deep breath.

Pastor Coker continued, "She also said Kyle Korte could have had something to do with it."

"Kyle! What would he have against Paula?"

"I have no idea," he replied. "She didn't say."

"Who's Kyle Korte?" Greg asked.

"He was in my class. He used to work construction for Aidan, but now he works at the fertilizer plant on the edge of town. He's currently rooming with Marty from the hardware store."

"Ah, I think I know who you're talking about."

Before the men could ask me any more questions about what I'd been doing, I said, "I'd better get some work done. Lots to do!"

"Don't forget to take the deposit to the bank." Pastor Coker headed back into his office.

I stifled a sigh. "I'll do it when I go to lunch."

I'd only forgotten to make the deposit one time, and since then he'd reminded me every week. I found it annoying, but he didn't do it to rub it in that I'd forgotten it once. He simply thought I would appreciate a reminder. Pastor Coker never did anything out of spite.

A few minutes before noon I retrieved the bank bag of cash and checks from the safe bolted to the floor in the pastor's office. I headed out the front door of the church and across the street to Cherry County Bank. The errand usually took me a while because my mom was a teller at the bank, and she always wanted to chat. But since she was out of town, I hoped to get in and out quickly.

That was not to be. Jeff Jenkins called out to me as I crossed the lobby on my way to the teller windows. I changed direction and headed to his office instead. He didn't often stop me to chat when I came in, as he was typically on the phone or with a customer. As the bank's vice president and loan officer, he was a busy man.

"You figure out who the killer is yet?" he asked.

"Nope," I said from the doorway.

"You're trying, though, right?"

I tried to give him a neutral look. "Maybe. Maybe not."

"Come on, Becky. I can read you like a book," my former boyfriend said. "What have you figured out so far?"

"I really can't say."

"Can't or won't?"

I shrugged. I wasn't sure I could trust him.

"All right, then," he said. "Be careful, okay?"

"I will," I said and headed back across the lobby.

Once the week's offering was safely in the church's bank account, I made my way down to The Check. The bell over the door jingled when I entered.

Callie waved at me from the cash register and jerked her head toward the back corner of the restaurant, where Veronica and Aunt Star sat across from each other in a booth. I threaded through the tables covered with red-and-white checked tablecloths and slid in next to Aunt Star, where I had a view of the door.

"Tell us what you've found out," Veronica said with no greeting.

"Hello to both of you," I said.

"Yes, hello," Veronica said. "Now, what have you learned?"

"I'll save the update from the newspaper office until Trixie gets here," I lowered my voice, "but here's what we learned about cyanide."

Trixie arrived while I was telling them what she'd told me at the library.

Callie stepped to the table to take our drink orders.

"Y'all here to talk about the murder?"

"Of course," I replied.

She glanced around to make sure nobody was sitting close by. Soon the place would be hopping, but it was still close enough to noon that the tables nearest us were empty.

"Karla was in here this morning with some friends—"

"Anyone from our class?" I interrupted as I pulled out my notebook and pen.

"Nope." She gave us a few names, but none of them could have anything to do with Paula's murder. "Anyway, I heard them mention Kyle's name a few times. I heard about what happened with him and Karla at the reunion. Doesn't surprise me on either side. I don't know what all the women were talking about, but there was something about an investment. I don't know what that would have to do with Kyle."

"What's strange," I tapped my pen on the notebook, "is Minnie Jensen called the church office and said she thought Kyle might have something to do with the murder. Not sure why she told us instead of the police."

"Maybe she told you *and* the police," Veronica said.

"I want to hear what else you might know about Kyle," Callie pointed her finger at me and swept it around to include everyone else, "but I need to take care of other customers for a while. And I'll get your drinks to you pronto." She hurried into the kitchen.

Aunt Star asked, "So why might Kyle have it in for Paula?"

"Or does he have something against Billy?" Trixie mused.

"Marty thinks Kyle's still in love with Karla," I informed them. "Maybe he killed Paula for her."

"But why not kill Billy instead?" Veronica held her hands palm up.

"Kyle could have thought that since Billy hurt the woman he—Kyle—loves, he'd hurt the woman Billy loves. A tit for tat kind of thing."

"That's a pretty big tit." Veronica turned a bright shade of red when the rest of burst out laughing and she realized what she'd said.

"What's so funny?" Callie set drinks in front of us.

Veronica shot eye daggers at the rest of us.

"You had to be here," I said.

"Suit yourself. You ready to place your food orders?"

We ordered, and she handed the ticket through the pass-through window for Bob, the diner's owner and cook, before heading to a table of new arrivals.

Trixie said, "What did you find out at the *Standard?*"

I turned to the page in my notebook with my notes about the photos. Before I could open my mouth, Trixie reached over and slammed the notebook shut on my hand.

"Ouch!" I yanked my hand back, slammed my elbow into the booth, and yelped. "What—"

Trixie gave me a piercing look and jerked her head to the side. I turned as Kyle pulled a chair from a nearby table, flipped it around backward at the end of our table, sat, and crossed his arms on top of the chair back in one fluid motion.

"What's happening, ladies? Interesting group you've got here."

I was too busy rubbing my elbow to answer.

"Just having lunch," Trixie said.

"And talking about the murder?" He raised his eyebrows.

"Do you have something you'd like to tell us?" Aunt Star tapped her fingernails on the table. "Or are you here merely to ask dumb questions and annoy us?"

I kicked her under the table, but she didn't flinch.

"I figured Miss Monahan here would be trying to solve this murder. She seems to do a better job at that than the police do."

I couldn't decide whether to be flattered by the praise or to be offended on Mitchell and Darren's behalf.

"Our police officers do a fine job," Aunt Star said testily. "And so does Beckett."

Veronica stuck her hand across the table toward Kyle. "I don't think I've had the pleasure of meeting you, young man. Veronica Coker."

Kyle winked at her and shook her hand. "Kyle Korte at your service."

"And what is that service?" she demanded without reacting to his wink. "Are you going to help us out here or what?"

He spread his hands wide. "Tell me what you need help with."

Callie approached us and put a fist on her cocked hip. "Kyle, you gonna order something, or are you only here to block my aisle?"

"What's with all you ladies today? I'm minding my own business and am getting attacked from every direction."

Callie raised an eyebrow at him.

"Okay, fine. I'll take a Coke. Will that do?"

"You're still blocking my aisle."

He craned his neck around to look behind him, and I took that opportunity to move my notebook onto the bench between me and Aunt Star.

Kyle said, "We can slide those two tables together and all sit there."

"No!" the rest of us shouted in unison.

Kyle pushed his hands palm down a few times. "Settle down now."

"Don't you tell us to settle down, Kyle Korte," Callie retorted. "Just get your business done here quickly and then move your tail on out."

"Got it."

Callie stalked away, and Kyle folded his arms across the back of his chair again. "Now," he cleared his throat and rotated his jaw, "where were we?"

"*We* were about to hear what *you* have to tell us about the murder," Trixie said.

"Ah, yes." He smirked. "I've got some dirt on Anita."

"*Dirt?* Really?" Aunt Star questioned.

"What's wrong with 'dirt'?"

"Give him a break, Aunt Star." I didn't want him giving up and not telling us what he knew.

"Thank you." He nodded regally at me.

I raised my eyebrows at him.

"Right," he said. "Anita didn't change jobs and move to St. Louis just because she felt like it." He paused, likely for dramatic effect, but the effect was more annoying than anything.

"And why didn't she feel like it?" Veronica asked.

"She was fired. Got a little too friendly with her boss's husband, so I heard."

Callie thunked Kyle's Coke on the table in front of him. "Who'd you hear that from?"

"Randy."

"How in the world would Randy Stouffer know that?" Trixie asked.

"You've got me. Maybe from Cheryl. Or from Barbara, who might have heard it from Frank."

Callie moved off to take another table's order.

"Speaking of Frank," I said, "I'd guess he knew this information, regardless of where Randy heard it." I swiveled my head so I could see everyone. "Do you think he told Darren and Mitchell? Are police required to share personal information about their family members that might incriminate them?"

"Frank would," Trixie said. "I'm not saying he'd easily betray a family member. But he's serious about the law. He'd tell everything he knew, if he remembered to tell it."

Veronica focused on Kyle. "Why do you think this is relevant?"

"If she was after one married man, she might be after another: Billy."

"You really think she'd kill to get him?" I couldn't imagine it.

"I don't know. I don't think any of us know." Kyle shook his head. "This is not the same Anita we knew when we were kids."

"You're right about that," Trixie acknowledged.

I still didn't think Anita had enough reason to kill Paula, but I wasn't about to tell Kyle that.

Kyle continued, "But since Anita is Frank's niece, I don't think they'd arrest her unless they have concrete evidence."

"They shouldn't arrest *anyone* without concrete evidence," I said. "But I do get your point. They'd make sure they were entirely certain with Anita. Same with Cheryl, since her mom works at the station."

"You think Cheryl had a reason to kill Paula?" Kyle asked.

I didn't, because she was clearly distressed after she found Paula's body, but I shrugged. "Do you?"

"She lives on a farm," he said, "which is an excellent place to find cyanide."

THIRTEEN

"HOW DO YOU KNOW it was cyanide that killed her?" I asked Kyle. I tried to sound shocked, since I wasn't supposed to know, either.

"It's out there," Kyle said enigmatically.

"Is it?" Aunt Star queried.

"Well, I heard about it, didn't I?"

"From who?" Veronica demanded.

"I'd rather not say."

I narrowed my eyes at him. "Anyway, tell us about farms and cyanide."

"Cyanide used to be a very common form of pesticide. Not as much now, but there's still a lot of it out there, especially on farms that have been around for a long time. And we know the Stouffers have farmed that land for generations. Their barn is at least fifty years old. Imagine all the junk that has accumulated in there."

"True," I said. "But that doesn't mean Cheryl did it."

"No, I'm simply saying she would have access."

"As would a lot of other people," Veronica added.

"There's a lot of old junk sitting around in Marty's shed," I said.

Kyle narrowed his eyes at me. "What are you saying?"

"I'm saying he had access, you had access, Karla had access, really anybody had access. That shed door is almost always open. Anybody could go in there at any time."

"But we don't have cyanide in the shed."

"How do you know?" Aunt Star asked.

Kyle looked thoughtful. "I guess I don't know."

"Exactly. That's my point," I said. "It could be anywhere on any of the farms around here, and we all know nobody locks anything." I paused. "How do you know so much about cyanide anyway?"

"At the fertilizer plant, we work with pesticides all the time. We can't use anything with cyanide these days, but the old guys talk about how much better it worked than anything we have now."

I sat back in my seat. How had none of us made the connection between Kyle and cyanide?

Callie appeared, balancing four plates on her arms. She jerked her head at Kyle. "Up. Out. Away. Whatever. Your time is up. Move your tush and the chair."

"Okay, okay." Kyle stood and swung the chair around to the table where it belonged. He whipped his wallet out and slapped two dollars on the table for his Coke and a generous tip. "See you ladies around."

After he sauntered off, Callie set our plates in front of us. "Did he tell you anything pertinent?"

"Only that cyanide could be found on any farm around here," Veronica said.

I hushed her, and she pressed her lips tightly together.

Callie crouched down and leaned her head over the table. "Cyanide?" she whispered. "Is that what killed her?"

"Yes, and if you hadn't heard that, how did Kyle know it?" I asked quietly.

Callie surveyed the diner and then took the chair Kyle had vacated, brought it back to our table, and sat. "Do we think Kyle could have done it?"

"He just talked about how they used to use pesticides with cyanide at the fertilizer plant. I'd guess there might still be some around." I also told her the theory that Kyle killed Paula for Karla while the others dug into their meals.

"Hmm. He might have done it for Karla," she said, "but it seems more likely Karla would have done it, if I had to choose between the two of them."

Trixie waved her fork at me. "You didn't get a chance to tell us about the photos."

I picked up my notebook from the seat, but it slipped from my hand and landed in my mashed potatoes and gravy.

"Oh, great." I lifted it and turned it over to see the damage.

Callie jumped up and was back with a rag in ten seconds. She took the notebook from me and wiped it clean. It would likely be left with a grease stain, but it was still usable.

I opened the notebook and told them about the photos as they ate silently.

"So Paula was drinking punch and talking to Kyle, Karla, Donna, and two or three others in the minutes leading up to her heading to the bathroom," I summarized. "And since we know cyanide can start working within minutes, it was most likely in her punch, since she's not eating in any of the pictures."

"But it was only in *her* punch, because nobody else even got sick, much less died." Trixie shoved a forkful of green beans into her mouth.

I waved my own fork at the others. "What I want to know is who gave her that cup of punch. Because the cyanide had to be added to her cup before she got it, or she or someone around her would almost certainly have noticed."

"Yes, the person who gave her the punch is the killer," Trixie said. "It's too bad the pictures don't show the handoff."

Someone across the diner called out for Callie, who stood and put the chair back in place. "Sorry, but I gotta get back to work."

"Let us know if you hear anything that might be important," I said.

She nodded and moved off across the room.

"Who took the pictures?" Veronica asked.

"Cheryl Stouffer," I said. "The woman Kyle was talking about who lives on a farm with her husband Randy. She's also the person who found Paula. Do you know her?"

"I don't think I've ever met her, but I know who she is. I'm acquainted with her parents-in-law."

"You're also familiar with her mother—Barbara Young at the police station," I stated.

"Yes." Veronica sniffed. "Barbara." The women's acquaintance hadn't started off well when they encountered each other at the station a few months earlier.

I tapped Trixie's plate. "Do you think Cheryl could have done it? She seemed legitimately traumatized after finding Paula in the bathroom."

Trixie shrugged. "I hate to think she could, but acting always came naturally to her."

She was right. Cheryl always got the lead female part in the school play, even when we were freshmen.

"We have a lot to think about." I picked up my fried chicken breast. "And I need to get this eaten and back to work or Pastor Coker and Greg will be even more curious about what I'm doing."

———

THE AFTERNOON BROUGHT NO more new information about the murder, and I didn't leave the church office again. After work I rushed home to change for Jazzercise. Aunt Star and I drove separately, so I could head over to Suzanne's afterward. When I pulled into the parking lot, Karla's car was there.

"Looks like Karla is joining us again," I said to Aunt Star as we got out of our cars. "I'll try to ask her a few questions."

"Be careful," Aunt Star warned. "If she's the killer, and she knows you're investigating, you could put yourself in danger."

"Kyle has probably already told her I'll be trying to find the killer. She probably suspected it anyway, since she knows about the last time. And no matter who the murderer is, they probably know I'll be involved."

"We need to make sure you don't go anywhere alone until this case is solved."

"I'll be fine," I insisted.

"Hmph."

Karla was stretching as we entered. I meandered over to her and started my own stretches. I usually waited to warm up until the whole class was ready, but I wanted to make our conversation seem more natural.

"Becky," she said as a greeting while she touched her toes.

"Karla," I returned. I stretched my arms above my head. "Didn't see you at The Blue Barn Saturday night."

"I spent the evening with my mom. She was pretty shaken up about Paula." She windmilled her arms. "As was I, of course."

"Of course," I parroted and attempted to touch my toes. I failed.

I thought I heard Karla snort, but I couldn't be sure.

"I didn't think you'd still be here." I did a handful of awkward jumping jacks.

"Chip went on home so he could get back to work, but I decided the kids and I would stick around until the funeral. Do you know when that will be? We didn't hear anything today."

"No. Yesterday Georgia said the police might be able to release the body today, but she wasn't sure. Since she didn't call the church, I guess that didn't happen. It'll still be at least a few more days, I'd say."

She nodded while jogging in place.

"Did you keep in touch with Paula?" I gave up on trying to

warm up and talk at the same time.

"Not really. I talked to Billy a few times about investments, but not Paula."

I wondered why she would mention the investments to me. And I was baffled by how she was neither breathing hard nor breaking a sweat.

"I was considering asking Billy about investing," I said. "He was always a numbers guy, so I'd guess he's good at his job."

Karla did a few lunges and avoided eye contact. "The church must be paying you well if you have money to spare."

"Just thinking toward the future," I said noncommittally. I tried doing a lunge but didn't get very far. Karla wasn't going to respond about Billy, so I tried another angle. "Or I could ask Anita about investing, since she does that now."

That time I did hear Karla snort.

"I wouldn't ask her to do anything other than keep her paws off my husband."

I was considering whether to comment on her hypocritical response when the leader called us all to attention and turned on the music. We started warming up to the sounds of "Neutron Dance."

———

I PULLED UP TO the curb outside Suzanne's house, after visiting the Dairy Queen drive-through. I knew it was silly to exercise and then immediately eat fast food, but I didn't have the time or the inclination to go home and fix something healthy.

I swapped my tennis shoes out for flip-flops, grabbed a duffel bag containing a change of clothes, my DQ bag, and my drink, and made my way to the side door of Suzanne's garage. I opened the door and sighed when the cool air hit me. I'd never known anyone else who air conditioned their garage, but I was thankful

Suzanne did.

She bustled over the moment she spotted me. "Tell me what you know."

"Know about what?"

"Don't give me that. You know what I'm talking about."

"Beckett!" a voice squealed from the other side of the flatbed trailer where the float was beginning to take shape.

Tiffani raced around the trailer and gave me a hug. Courtney, the new girl, shyly followed her over. I held my arm out to let her know it was okay for her to hug me too. She gave me a quick hug and then looked at the floor, which was her norm. I hoped I could get her to come out of her shell a little more.

"Girls, get back to work, please," Suzanne ordered.

"Yes, Miss LaHaye." Courtney walked back around to the other side of the trailer, where a group of women and girls were making tissue-paper red, white, and blue flowers.

"Sure, whatever," Tiffani said with a huff as she followed Courtney.

"That girl ..." Suzanne trailed off. I was proud of her for managing to keep the rest of that thought to herself.

"Is it okay if I use your bathroom to change? I didn't take time to go home after Jazzercise."

"Sure. But first, what do you know about the murder?"

"Beckett, I'm glad to see you," another voice interrupted us.

Maggie approached us. Since she had wanted to avoid Suzanne at church the previous morning, I was surprised to see her. But Maggie was a woman who always followed through on her commitments, so it made sense she would be at Suzanne's, if she'd signed up to help with the float.

"Maggie!" I stepped away from Suzanne to greet her. Out of the corner of my eye, I saw Suzanne sigh. "What can I help you with?"

"Come on over here and I'll show you." She headed toward

the front of the trailer, where she was using a staple gun to attach red, white, and blue bunting along the edge.

"Thanks," I whispered, when we were out of Suzanne's earshot.

"It seemed you needed rescuing."

"I did. I also need to change my clothes. I'll be right back to help."

I set my food and drink down and hurried into the house to change out of my sweaty workout clothes.

When I returned to the garage, I avoided eye contact with Suzanne and made a beeline for Maggie. Since I already knew she hadn't been in close touch with Paula, I didn't ask her any questions related to the murder. I ate my burger and fries with one hand while holding the bunting in place with the other. We mostly worked in companionable silence or sang along with the radio, which was tuned to the local country station. For some reason, Suzanne thought country music was more wholesome than "that terrible rock music," even though so many country songs talked about cheating and drinking.

I took over with the staple gun and was humming along to George Strait's new song "The Fireman" when Maggie said in a low voice, "Right before I came over here, Mom called. She had talked to Aunt Georgia, who said the police questioned Cheryl Stouffer."

My head snapped up. "What? Really?"

"Yeah, I couldn't believe it either."

"Did she say why they were questioning her?" I fired a staple through the cloth.

"She didn't know. Frank asked Aunt Georgia and Billy to come to the police station so they could tell them about the coroner's report. When my aunt got there, she gathered that Cheryl had just left, as Barbara was yelling at Darren and calling him some pretty choice names."

"Yikes."

"Indeed."

"What did your aunt say about the coroner's report?"

"The police told them not to say anything about the cause of death. Really makes you wonder, doesn't it? It's so strange they don't want us to know how she died, even though everybody knows it was probably poison, because they took everyone's drinks at the reunion."

If she didn't know the poison was cyanide, I wondered again how Kyle found out.

"I think they want to keep it under wraps for now." I fired another staple. "Because that might help them find the killer. Possibly they're hoping that person will slip up and mention exactly how she died, when they shouldn't know."

Like Kyle did.

"Darren told Billy and Aunt Georgia they can plan the funeral now. I guess you'll help with that."

"Me? Why?"

Maggie gave me a funny look.

"Oh, yeah." I grinned sheepishly. "Because I work at the church. Sorry. Don't know where my brain is."

The garage suddenly went silent, except for Alabama singing "40 Hour Week." I stood from where I'd been kneeling next to the trailer and immediately knew why nobody was talking. Darren, in full uniform, stood in the doorway. He spotted me and headed my way.

FOURTEEN

DARREN LEANED DOWN TO my ear and said so only I could hear, "Everything's okay. Act natural and follow my lead."

More loudly he said, "We have a few more questions for you about the reunion. Can you come with me?"

I nodded, handed the staple gun to Maggie, grabbed my duffel bag, and followed him out.

Before the door closed behind us, Suzanne's voice rang out, "Well, I never!"

Darren and I grinned at each other for a second until we both realized I didn't know the real reason he was there. He took me by the elbow and hurried me away from the door. Once we were next to my car, he said, "I may have been fibbing when I said everything is okay."

My hand went to my heart. "Aunt Star?"

I immediately felt faint. He must have seen it in my eyes, because he reached out and gripped my arms.

"She's fine! Every*body's* okay. That's the important thing. I should have led with that. Sorry. Anyway," he took a deep breath, "someone broke into your house this evening."

"Oh, my word! Was Aunt Star there?"

He closed his eyes for a second. "No. I'm screwing this all up. I'm not used to giving people bad news. Frank is much better at it than I am."

"I would sure hope so," I said with a wan smile, but I patted his arm.

133

"No, your aunt wasn't there when it happened. After your exercise class, she stopped by your parents' house to water the garden. When she got home, she parked in the garage as usual, but when she opened the door into the kitchen, the place was a mess. She didn't turn around and leave like any normal person would, but instead she searched the house. After she didn't find anyone, *then* she called us. Which should have been the first thing she did—from somewhere else."

His head jerked up, his eyes left mine, and he said loudly, "Everything's fine out here, Suzanne."

I turned to see her wave and head back toward the garage.

"Let's get out of here." He bent down to my eye level. "Are you okay to drive?"

"Yes, we don't have far to go. Our house or the station?"

"Your house. Detective Crowe is over there with Starla."

"You can call him Mitchell, you know."

"I really shouldn't get into the habit."

Darren was nothing if not professional. He opened the door of my Pinto, flipped the driver's seat forward to check the back seat, reached through and locked the passenger door, and finally ushered me in. "You'll want to start locking your car. And don't ever leave your purse in it."

I nodded sheepishly, put my key in the ignition, and cranked the engine.

Darren said, "Wait a second for me to get into my car, and I'll follow you home. By the way, don't park in the garage when you get there." He locked my door and slammed it shut.

Though I was upset about what had happened and concerned about my aunt, I also couldn't help being anxious about my appearance. I was about to see Mitchell, but I was wearing a ratty old T-shirt, I had removed all my makeup before Jazzercise, and I didn't smell all that fresh. I determined to put all of that out of my head, though. The important thing was my aunt was safe.

I was surprised Mitchell's car wasn't in front of the house when we arrived, but when Darren and I entered through the front door, he was on the couch. I raced over to my aunt in her easy chair, leaned down, and gave her an awkward hug.

Then I turned to Mitchell. "Where's your car?"

"Hello, and nice to see you, too, Beckett." His eyes slowly traveled down to my feet and back up, and I felt a blush follow his gaze. "Darren and I rode over here together. Officers Nichols and Park have come and gone. They took fingerprints and took some evidence with them."

"Hi. Sorry. I'm a little flustered," I said before crossing to the entrance into the kitchen, which I discovered was spotless. I turned back into the living room. "Where's the mess?"

"I already picked up everything in these two rooms," Aunt Star explained. "Everywhere else is still a disaster, though."

I plopped down next to Mitchell on the couch, and he patted my leg. He left his hand there, but when Darren cleared his throat, Mitchell slid it off onto the couch, but he kept his pinky in contact with my thigh.

Darren drew the curtains across the picture window and then sat on the pink and baby blue love seat under it. He pulled out his notebook, as did Mitchell.

"Before you start asking questions, can I ask a few?" I asked.

"Sure."

"My first one is: What the heck happened here?"

Mitchell's head snapped toward Darren. "You didn't tell her?"

"I told her someone broke in—not any of the details. Suzanne was getting nosy, so we needed to get out of there." Darren turned to me. "One of the dining room windows was open, so it must have been unlocked."

"We rarely go in there, and I don't think I've ever opened a window in that room," I said.

My aunt said, "About a month ago I opened all the windows

to air the place out. I guess I forgot to lock that one."

"What did they take?" I asked.

"Nothing, according to your aunt," Mitchell said. "And nothing is broken."

"If they didn't take or break anything, then why were they here?" I sank back into the couch cushions.

"Likely to scare you," Darren said.

"Oh. I guess that makes sense."

"Why does it make sense?" He gave me an intense look. "Why would someone try to scare you?"

"I maybe am doing a little, teeny-weeny bit of investigating." I placed my thumb and pointer finger a half inch apart.

"A little, teeny-weeny bit, huh?" He sighed.

"I know. Don't start. And don't tell me you didn't know I couldn't sit around and wait to see what happened."

"I seem to recall you promising you wouldn't try to solve this."

I held up a finger. "One, I didn't promise." I held up a second finger. "Two, I said I wouldn't *try*. I'm not trying. I'm doing."

Darren threw his head back and groaned.

"Hon—" Aunt Star fake coughed. "Darren, you really should have known better."

Mitchell placed his hand back on my leg. "I really wish you wouldn't do this. It's not safe."

"It's not safe for you either," I retorted.

"I wear a gun." He pointed to the handgun strapped to his waist. "And I'm trained to investigate murders."

"I've never seen you wear a gun like that before," I said.

"It's usually hidden beneath my clothes, but I needed it to be easily accessible tonight when I got here. We didn't know exactly what we were dealing with."

"Just so you know," Darren said to me, "we took all your food. You'll need to wash anything that holds food or drink. I'd even toss out your toothbrushes, toothpaste, and mouthwash."

My eyes widened. "You think the killer is trying to poison us, too?"

"We don't know," Mitchell said. "We'll test some of the food to check."

"Do you have any more questions?" Darren asked me.

"Who's your main suspect?"

He let out an exaggerated sigh.

"I think I should be aware of who to watch out for, since someone is obviously out to get me. And not just me—Aunt Star is in this too."

She sputtered in response. I didn't mean to throw her under the bus, but Darren would be more likely to spill the beans if he knew she was in as much danger as I was.

"I know," Darren said.

My aunt's jaw dropped. "You do?"

"I'm not dumb," he replied. "If one of you knows something, the other knows it within hours. I have met the two of you."

I caught my aunt's eye, and we couldn't help but grin at each other. If anyone asked who my best friend was, I would say Trixie, but my aunt and I were even closer these days. I liked to think that would be the case even if we didn't live together.

"Back to the question at hand," I said to Darren, "care to tell us who we should keep an eye out for?"

"These names can't go beyond this room," he commanded. "Not even to Trixie or Mrs. Coker."

I hesitated. "But they're helping us investigate. We need to keep them safe as well."

Darren closed his eyes for a moment. "Good grief. Anyone else involved in your shenanigans?"

"They're not shenanigans!" I protested. "I think you may have forgotten I'm the one who caught Aidan's killer."

"I'll give you that. Now promise me."

"Fine. I promise." I did think it was a promise I'd be able to keep.

Mitchell said, "Right now we're looking closely at Cheryl Stouffer, Karla Bright, and Kyle Korte."

"It can't be Karla," I said immediately.

"What? Why?" Mitchell turned his body sideways on the couch to face me.

"She was at Jazzercise with us." I nodded toward Aunt Star. "I don't know how long you were at my parents' house, but I doubt it was long enough to give her time to break in here. Plus, she would have figured we were going straight home afterward anyway. It can't be her," I reiterated. "At least she wasn't the one who broke in, which likely also means she wasn't the murderer."

Mitchell wrote something in his notebook. "Was anyone else from the reunion at your exercise thing?"

My lips twitched because he couldn't bring himself to say the word "Jazzercise."

He continued, "And did you see anyone else from the reunion between the time you left there and when you got home?"

I stuck my pinky nail in my mouth and closed my eyes as I recalled the events of the past few hours.

"Nobody else was at Jazzercise," I said.

"I saw Randy Stouffer's pickup when I was on my way here from Minda's," Aunt Star said.

"Minda?" Mitchell's brow furrowed.

My eyes popped open. "My mom."

He wrote that in his notebook.

Darren peppered Aunt Star with questions. "Where did you see the truck? What direction was it heading? Could you see who was driving?"

"It was parked at the curb in front of Donna Jenkins' house."

"Randy and Donna?" I asked. "I don't see that happening."

"Maybe Cheryl was driving Randy's truck," she replied.

"Maybe so, and she was trying to use visiting Donna as an alibi for breaking in here." That didn't seem likely, but you never knew.

"This is great info. What else do you remember?" Mitchell poised his pen above his notebook.

Aunt Star's mention of a pickup jogged a memory. "Kyle's Jeep was a couple cars behind me in the Dairy Queen drive-through," I said.

"What time were you there?" Darren asked.

"Right after Jazzercise." I crossed my legs under me. "What about Anita? Is she not a suspect?"

"No clear motive. She readily admitted to having an interest in Billy, but she claimed she was biding her time until he and Paula got divorced. She said it was inevitable."

"That's exactly what I was thinking," I replied. "Hey, we saw Kyle at lunch today, and he knew about the cyanide. How would he know that?"

The two men's eyes snapped toward each other and then focused on me.

"You haven't told anybody about it?" Darren narrowed his eyes.

"Nope."

"Me, either," Aunt Star said.

"You know Trixie would never tell." I didn't mention that Veronica also knew and spilled it to Callie at lunch. But I still didn't think it would be her. "I also talked to Paula's cousin Maggie, and she said Georgia wouldn't even tell her own sister—Maggie's mom—how Paula died, so I know Georgia hasn't said anything."

"Would Scott tell anyone?" Mitchell asked.

"The man only speaks about two hundred words a day," I said. "It didn't come from him."

"The cyanide is not public knowledge." Darren tapped his pen on his leg.

Aunt Star said, "You've got a leak at the station, gentlemen."

"Or Kyle's the killer," I said. "Or has talked to the killer, whether knowingly or not."

"What about Billy?" Aunt Star asked.

"Please don't let it be Billy." I forgot about Kyle for the moment.

"We've eliminated him from the suspect list," Darren said.

"Why?"

"We just have," he said in a clipped tone.

He was done giving us information then. We wouldn't get anything out of him about why they questioned Cheryl or why they suspected Kyle. And I wasn't about to bring up the topic of the photos for fear I'd give away that I'd seen them. I didn't want to put Edna in a tight spot.

"It would be silly for Billy to kill his wife in such a public place," I said. "If he wanted to kill her, he would choose a more private setting."

"Killing her at the reunion would provide a lot of alternate suspects, though," Aunt Star responded.

Darren and Mitchell didn't chime in. If they were going to listen to our theories, I figured I'd try one more time to discover theirs.

"Why did you question Cheryl today? What's her motive?"

Darren flipped his notebook shut and stood. "Can't tell you that. Ready, Detective Crowe?"

Mitchell pushed himself off the couch. "Let me check that all the windows are locked." He headed into the kitchen.

I stood. "My car's not in the garage. Can I pull it in now?" I asked Darren.

"Yes. I didn't know if they'd be finished collecting evidence when we got here, but now let's get it locked up inside."

Aunt Star jumped to her feet. "Give me your keys and I'll do it. Darren, come with me. You'll need to keep me safe."

When he turned to the door, she wiggled her eyebrows at me and nodded in Mitchell's direction. I took her cue, pulled my keys out of my purse, and tossed them to her. She caught them, pulled Darren out the front door, and closed it behind her.

FIFTEEN

MITCHELL HAD HEADED UPSTAIRS, so I followed him. He came out of my bedroom as I reached the top step.

"I didn't see anything in there, I promise." He crossed a finger over his heart while struggling to keep a straight face.

I stepped around him and my mouth fell open. All my dresser drawers had been dumped out, and my underwear and bras were scattered over every surface. My face warmed as Mitchell spun me around, pulled me flush to him, and rested his hands on my hips. His gun pressed into my side, but I didn't complain.

"Looks like we're alone for a minute." He leaned down for a brief but heated kiss.

"I thought we couldn't do this," I murmured against his lips as I gripped the front of his shirt.

"Short lapse of judgment." He kissed my forehead, gently unwrapped my hands from his shirt, and pressed them flat against his chest. "Don't want anyone to wonder why my shirt is wrinkled all of a sudden." His brown eyes twinkled. "Speaking of clothes, I'm a fan of your shorts."

I hadn't felt self-conscious wearing the skintight biker shorts and oversized T-shirt at Suzanne's, but now I blushed wildly.

"Detective Crowe, you ready?" Darren's voice boomed up the stairs.

"Go on down," I whispered. "I'll check the other windows."

"Almost done!" Mitchell called out to Darren. Then he said in a low voice, "One more lapse first." He cupped my face with both hands and kissed me again.

"You're cute when you blush," he informed me before thundering down the stairs.

"Bye!" I called after him in a weak voice. Then I gathered my strength and called out, "Bye, Darren. Thanks!"

His voice filtered up to me. "No problem. Be careful. See you later."

I didn't go downstairs to see them out, because I knew my face would betray me. Instead, I leaned against my bedroom door frame and surveyed the mess. The front door slammed, and my heart started pounding, but not because of Mitchell. It finally sank in that someone broke into our house and pilfered through our belongings. Some unknown person touched my underwear! I shivered.

"My room is even worse," Aunt Star said from behind me.

I let out a shriek and turned to her. "I didn't hear you coming up the stairs."

"Sorry." She uncharacteristically wrapped her arms around me. "And I'm sorry this happened. Maybe if I hadn't stopped by your parents' house ..."

I leaned back and searched her eyes. "This was *not* your fault. It was not my fault. It's nobody's fault but the person who did it."

She let go of me. "You're right. You want help cleaning this up?"

I turned around and surveyed the mess. "I'm going to need to wash all these clothes before I wear them again. Thankfully it looks like they didn't touch my closet. I won't have any clean underwear, though." I grimaced.

"Maybe you'll run true to form, and you'll have a load of clean laundry in the dryer," she said wryly.

I laughed. "You're probably right."

"Let's send all this to the basement, and then we'll go check."

While she brought piles of clothes from my bedroom into the bathroom, I chucked them down the laundry chute. Then we did the same with her clothes. Unfortunately, both her dresser and her closet had been hit, so she was left with nothing to wear.

We trooped to the basement, where we discovered I did have a clean load of clothes in the dryer. I let it tumble for a minute and then loaded it into a laundry basket while Aunt Star picked through the mountain of clothes beneath the chute and started a load in the washing machine.

"Next up: filling the dishwasher." I hefted the laundry basket against my hip and led the way upstairs. "You want to borrow some of my clothes for tonight?"

"Yes, please."

I knew she'd make sure a load or two of laundry was finished before she went to work the next day, though. She wouldn't be caught dead wearing any of my clothes in public. Plus, they'd be a few sizes too big for her petite frame.

———

THE NEXT MORNING, while I drank Diet Coke straight from the can, I asked my aunt, "Why do you think nobody has called us to ask what happened here last night?"

She swallowed a bite of a granola bar she'd dug out of her purse. "Darren said they didn't use their lights or sirens, because they didn't want to cause a stir. If anybody saw them here, they probably assume it was routine questioning about the murder. Plus, it's not uncommon for Darren's car to be here anyway."

I tapped my fingernails on the table. "They didn't say this, but I'm guessing they don't want us telling anyone what happened."

"You're probably right. Please stop tapping your fingernails."

I stilled my fingers. "I'm going to tell Trixie and Veronica, though. Because Kyle knows they're also looking into this. They need to be on guard."

She nodded. "You doing okay?"

I blew out a breath. "I hate to admit this, but the break-in has shaken me up more than the murder did. The thought that somebody was in our house going through our stuff without our permission gives me the willies." I shuddered.

"Me, too."

"You're not going to tell my mom about this, are you?" I poured my cup of coffee.

"Are you serious?" She snorted. "Of course not."

"I'm only asking." I paused. "You were up earlier than usual this morning." The creaking floorboards in the hall had briefly woken me before it was even light outside.

"I couldn't sleep, so I figured I'd finish cleaning up the guest room and dining room to try to remove the reminders of what happened."

"Did it help?"

"No. I got another load of laundry done, though."

"It's going to take us a while to get through it all."

"What are you up to today?"

I stood and took a last gulp of soda before answering. "Church and then Suzanne's to work on the float again. And I'll go to the store at some point to buy some groceries. I don't know what to do as far as the investigation goes. I am a little wary now."

"That was the killer's plan. Don't let them win." She paused. "But I feel the same. We need to be very careful."

———

I WAS TYPICALLY THE first to arrive at the church in the morning, but several cars sat in the parking lot when I pulled in, including Suzanne's Cadillac, Georgia's white Chevy Caprice, and a black four-door car I knew I should recognize but couldn't quite place. I let myself in the door from the parking lot, and piano music drifted down the hall from the choir room. A quick glance as I passed the open door revealed Suzanne at the upright piano pounding out "When We All Get to Heaven." I rushed past before she could sense my presence.

"Beckett, it's about time you showed up," Veronica said when I entered the office.

Georgia looked at her watch. "I think she's right on time."

Veronica ignored her and I tried to see past them into the pastor's office.

"Now," Veronica said, "the funeral is tomorrow morning, and the visitation is tonight, so we've got a lot to do. The visitation will be here at the church, since they're predicting storms this afternoon and evening, and the funeral home isn't going to be able to hold everyone. Nobody wants to wait in line in the pouring rain."

I dropped my purse on top of a pile of papers on my desk. "We'll get it done. Who's in there?" I pointed toward Pastor Coker's office, from which several male voices emanated.

"Billy, Tommy, and Wayne Cooper. They're working on the order of service for the funeral," Veronica explained.

Wayne Cooper was the owner and director of Cooper's Funeral Home, the only funeral home in town. I had forgotten that Georgia said her son Tommy wanted to speak at his sister's funeral. I figured he and Pastor Coker would share duties.

"Suzanne's working on the music," Veronica added unnecessarily.

"I wish you had called and asked me to come in early. But why the rush?"

Georgia said, "Tommy needs to get back home for a Fourth of July event at his church. And we all want it to be done and behind us." She paused, and I noticed the dark circles under her eyes. "Not that it'll really help." Her eyes welled up.

I gave her a hug. "Are we doing a meal for the family here at the church?"

"Of course," Veronica said. "Instead of doing it after the funeral tomorrow, it will be tonight from 4:30 to 6:15, with visitation starting at 6:30."

"We'd better get on it, then," I said.

"I already started the phone tree," Veronica said, "so the church ladies will all soon know to start cooking."

"Excellent. Let's go get the fellowship hall and kitchen ready. We'll need to make some room in the refrigerators. Food will likely begin arriving in a few hours." I knew I'd need some help, though. "Do you think it's okay if I ask Greg to come in?"

Veronica nodded. "We could use his help, even if it is his day off. No need to bother Harold about it. Call and see if he's available, and we'll head on down to the kitchen."

I called Greg and filled him in. He didn't have any set plans for the day, so he readily agreed to help.

"Can you stop and get several bags of ice on your way in?" I asked before ending the call. "Grab some petty cash from the safe to reimburse yourself when you get here."

"Will do."

The choir room was silent as I approached it, and I hoped Suzanne had left the building. I was not in luck. I found her in the fellowship hall with the other ladies, discussing table decorations.

"I think white tablecloths on the serving tables, and some silk flowers scattered on the rest of the tables," Georgia said.

"Oh, no, honey," Suzanne replied. "We can do better than that. Follow me." She bustled toward the closet that housed the table decorations at the back of the large room.

The other ladies followed her, and none of them noticed me in the doorway, so I headed into the kitchen.

I hauled the large garbage can over to the smaller of the two refrigerators and opened the door. The space was mostly filled with generic-brand cans of soda for the youth group but also contained a few foil-covered serving dishes. I peeled back the foil on one to reveal a half-eaten red JELL-O and banana salad. Undoubtedly it would be replaced by an identical dish within hours. I upended the bowl over the trash can and shook it until the JELL-O jiggled out and fell with a plop. I was cleaning old food and condiments out of the other fridge when Greg arrived with two bags of ice.

"Put those in the deep freeze, will you?" I asked. "Thanks. And hi!"

He laughed and headed around the kitchen island to the pantry closet containing the freezer. "Hi right back."

I called out to him, "If the fridges start to fill up, can I move some of the sodas out?"

"I don't care if you take them out now." He came back out of the pantry. "Let me help you."

"No use taking them out until we know we need the room, but stack them up so they take up as little space as possible."

"Aye-aye, captain!" he joked.

I rolled my eyes. He frowned at my response, so I grinned and playfully punched him in the arm, which made him perk back up. I couldn't help but mentally compare his maturity level with Mitchell's. There really was no comparison. Greg was still an insecure boy in many ways, but Mitchell was one hundred percent man. I closed my eyes as I remembered that very man's lips on mine.

"Earth to Beckett!"

I opened my eyes to Greg waving his hand in front of my face.

"I thought I'd lost you to another planet there for a second."

Not another planet, just another man.

He helped me finish preparing the kitchen, and then I opened the accordion doors along the pass-through counter into the fellowship hall. The three older ladies had set up two of the long, folding tables, which overflowed with various decorations.

Greg peered through the opening. "Looks like we need to get the rest of the tables and chairs set up."

We had used the space for a rather elaborate youth group game the previous Wednesday night and failed to set the tables and chairs back up when we were finished.

"Why didn't we get the boys to do it after youth group last week?"

He shrugged. "We should have, but we didn't know we'd be having a dinner here this week. You up for it?"

"As much as I'll ever be. Let's get it done."

We headed into the fellowship hall, and while we were setting up the first table, Pastor Coker and the other men walked in. Billy rushed across the room to take over for me, and the other two made their way to the wall where the other tables stood waiting.

I thanked them for helping and approached the women.

"You get all the police's questions answered last night?" Suzanne asked me.

"What questions?" Veronica picked up a silk flower bouquet and inspected it.

I needed to tell Veronica what had happened, but I couldn't do that with the other ladies present, so I simply said, "Yes, they had a few more questions for me. No big deal."

"Mmhm." Suzanne peered at me through narrowed eyes. "I'll tell you what might be a big deal, though." She quickly turned to Georgia, as if wondering if she should continue. After a few seconds she said in a low voice, "The police questioned Cheryl Stouffer yesterday." She reached over and squeezed Georgia's arm. "I thought you should know."

"I already knew," Georgia said. "But go on."

"You knew?" Suzanne seemed annoyed that she wasn't the first to share the news. "What do you know about it?"

"Nothing, really. I only know it happened." Georgia wouldn't look Suzanne in the eye.

"Well, did you also know the police searched the Stouffers' barn?" Suzanne sounded mighty pleased with herself.

"Noooo," Georgia and I both said.

"What do you think they were looking for?" Suzanne asked.

"Good question," I replied.

"Very strange," Veronica said.

"Hmmm," Georgia added.

I mentally hugged them both for not spilling the beans. I also noted none of us technically lied to Suzanne.

Suzanne narrowed her eyes at me. "You're not even going to take a guess?"

"Oh! Well, they could have been looking for the murder weapon."

"Which was ...?"

"You tell me," I said noncommittally.

"I just wish they'd find that monster," Georgia said, eyes flashing. "It makes me extremely uneasy that my girl's killer is still out there somewhere—probably right here in town."

"Surely the police will figure it out soon." I put an arm around her shoulders. "Sounds like they're hot on the trail."

Veronica nodded. "Yes, shouldn't be long now, I'd say."

I turned to face the room, which had now nearly filled with tables. I was glad they men had come, because it would have taken Greg and me a lot longer working alone. I didn't know if Georgia would leave with Tommy or if she welcomed the distraction of helping set up at the church, but if she was going to leave, I had a limited amount of time to get Veronica away from Suzanne without suspicion.

"Mrs. Coker," I said, "why don't you and I go make sure everything is in order in the sanctuary, while these ladies keep working in here?" I gave her foot a nudge so she'd know I wanted to get her alone.

"That's a great plan." She said to the others, "We'll be back in a jiffy," and strode purposefully toward the door.

I hurried after her.

"I'm glad to get you alone," she said once we were in the hallway. "I have something to tell you."

SIXTEEN

"SAME HERE," I SAID to Veronica. "You tell me what you know first."

We continued down the hallway toward the sanctuary, as we truly did need to get it ready.

"I knew about them searching the Stouffers' barn. They also searched the shed where Marty and Kyle live."

"Wow. How did you hear that?"

"I happened to be passing the Stouffers' and saw the police cars there. Then I wondered where else they might be searching, so I waited an hour and went for another drive. That's when I spotted them at the other place."

We stepped into the sanctuary. Everything was in its normal place, but we'd need to move a few things to make room for the casket and for the family to stand to receive guests. The table in front of and below the pulpit where the offering plates sat was too heavy for us to move, but we cleared it off.

"What did you need to tell me?" she asked.

"Somebody broke into our house last night!"

"Oh, Beckett!" she exclaimed. I thought she might even hug me, but she didn't. "Are you okay? Do they know who did it? How haven't I heard about this?"

I explained what happened and that the police didn't want to make a big deal about it. "But I wanted to make sure you know, because there are some people who know you're helping me. You could be in danger, too."

She stood up as straight as possible. "They wouldn't dare mess with a pastor's wife!"

"You sure about that?"

She sank down onto the front pew. "No. Thanks for telling me." She paused. "I wonder if I should tell Harold."

I didn't know if she was asking for my opinion, but I said, "That's up to you. But at this point, it might be for the best if you do."

"That will be the end of me being part of the investigation."

She actually pouted, and I struggled not to laugh.

"I can still keep you informed," I said.

"I guess that will have to do." She stood. "Let's finish up in here and get back down to the fellowship hall."

We put away the signs announcing our upcoming Vacation Bible School and were placing boxes of tissues on the floor at the end of each pew when Suzanne announced her entrance with, "What's taking you ladies so long?"

I rolled my eyes and turned toward her. "Where's Georgia?"

"Tommy took her home. She wants to spend as much time as she can with her grandkids before they head home tomorrow."

"Ah. That makes sense. Can you help us move the offering table?"

The three of us managed to shift the heavy wooden table off to the side to leave room for the casket.

"I'd better get back to the office," I said. "I'm sure we'll get lots of calls all day." I had answered a few from the kitchen phone while Greg and I were working.

"Yes, you go on," Veronica said. "And I'm sure Suzanne has some more preparation to do before tomorrow."

I turned back to Suzanne before exiting the sanctuary. "What about the float? Will we have time to get it done since we can't work on it tonight?"

"We'll finish up tomorrow evening before and after church,"

she said. "I hope we can get it all done."

"How about I gather up all the youth group girls to go over and help, maybe during youth group time tomorrow night?" I knew Greg wouldn't mind, under the circumstances.

She sighed in relief. "Yes, let's do that. Thanks. That's a load off my mind."

I hurried back to the office. The phone was ringing when I entered, and neither of the men were anywhere to be seen. I grabbed the phone on Greg's desk, since it was closest to me.

"Beckett, I'm glad it's you. This is Darren, by the way."

"Yes, I did recognize the voice."

"Oh. Is the church hosting a dinner for the funeral, like usual?"

"Yes, but it's tonight before the visitation, not tomorrow after the funeral." I circled Greg's desk and sat in his chair.

"It's *tonight?* Has anyone brought food yet?"

"No. Why?"

He hesitated a moment. "Can you meet me at your house in ten minutes?"

"I guess so. I'll have to get someone else to answer the phone while I'm gone."

"No need to do that. You won't be gone long."

He was acting very strangely, but instead of questioning him, I said, "Got it. See you soon."

Darren's subterfuge piqued my interest. He obviously didn't want anyone to know I was talking to him or even leaving the church. I grabbed my purse and took the long way around the building to my car, to try to avoid anyone inside seeing me.

When I reached home, I opened the garage door, and Aunt Star's car was inside, which was strange for the time of day. I pulled in and was about to hit the remote button to close the overhead door when I spotted Darren's car pulling into the driveway behind me via the rearview mirror. He was out of his car and into the garage before I stepped out of my own car. He tapped the garage door button on the wall and motioned me inside the house.

"Why all the cloak and dagger?" I asked.

Aunt Star was waiting at the kitchen table. "Yeah, what's going on?"

Darren and I joined her at the table.

"Since both of you were in a place where someone else could be listening in on your conversation, I decided we needed to meet in person. I also don't fully trust everyone at the department right now, so it's best I not mention this there, either. Nobody but Detective Crowe knows I'm here."

"Ugh, just call him Mitchell already."

Darren pursed his lips at me but didn't reply.

"Becks," my aunt warned.

"What? I'm just saying." I turned to Darren. "Tell us what you need, so I can get back to the church before anybody misses me."

"I'm concerned about this meal," he said.

"Why?"

"Remember what happened the last time there was a group meal in this town—with some of the same people?"

I tapped my fingers on the tabletop. "So what do you want us to do—tell them to cancel it?"

"No, we don't have a good enough reason to do that."

"We could try," I insisted.

"We can't hold the town hostage until we catch the killer," he said. "But we do need to use caution."

"Then what's your plan?"

"You two, Trixie, and Mrs. Coker need to be solely in charge of the food and drink. Don't let anyone else in the kitchen. You receive it from people as they drop it off. If that person, or anyone close to them, was at the reunion, do *not* serve the food.

Set it aside in that little pantry off the kitchen."

"But couldn't someone taint any of the food once it's on the serving tables?"

"There will be no serving tables. Set out the dishes on the counter between the kitchen and the fellowship hall, and you will serve the food to them. Like at the school cafeteria."

"But we've already got the room set up with serving tables."

"Change it."

"Whoa, now." Aunt Star crossed her arms over her chest. "We are not your suspects in an interrogation room. Don't treat us like it."

Darren sighed, leaned back in his chair, and clasped his hands behind his head. "Sorry. I'm a little on edge about this. I don't want any more dead bodies popping up, and that dinner is the prime place for it to happen."

"I get that," I said. "We'll do what we need to do to keep things safe. I'll make it work. And we can take care of the drink issue by serving cans of soda. We have plenty of it already."

"Thank you." He put his elbows on the table and pointed at me with both hands. "Don't you eat a single thing brought to the dinner." He moved his focus to Aunt Star. "Or you. Do you hear me?"

"Don't you ever boss me around again, Darren Turley, but yes, I hear you," my aunt said.

"Me, too," I said.

"Good. The same goes for Trixie and Mrs. Coker. The four of you would be the killer's primary targets right now."

I nodded and stood. "I need to call Trixie and tell her what's happening before I head out. I'll tell Veronica when I get back to the church, if I can get her away from Suzanne."

Aunt Star grabbed her keys and headed toward the door. "I need to get back to the office for a house closing, but I can head over to the church after noon." The door slammed behind her.

"I'll wait and make sure you get back to the church safely," Darren said. "Not that I'm not also worried about your aunt, but you're the one they'd most likely come after."

I dialed Trixie's number on the kitchen phone and then stretched the cord over to my seat at the table. Darren picked at his fingernails while I filled Trixie in on our plan. I was tempted to reach over and slap his hands.

When I hung up the phone, I said, "She'll be there as soon as she can drop the kids off with her mom."

"Excellent." He led the way to the door, and we headed out.

I groaned aloud when I spotted Suzanne's car still parked in the church lot. How was I going to get Veronica away from her to explain the plan? More importantly, how was I going to keep Suzanne out of the kitchen for the rest of the day?

As I made my way back around the church to the door next to the office, I began formulating a plan. When I discovered Greg was the only person in the office, that cemented it. I needed to let him in on what was happening.

"I'm glad you're here." I collapsed into my chair and pulled at the front of my shirt a few times to try to cool down after my brief walk in the heat.

Greg beamed at me. "And why are you glad?"

"Because I need your help. And I need you to keep the reasons a secret. And I need you to not lecture me. Can you do all those things?"

He pulled a chair up to the other side of my desk. "I'm at your service. Tell me what you need."

I told him about the cyanide and the plans for dinner. "During the dinner, can you help keep everyone else out of the kitchen?"

"Yes, but I can't be two places at once."

"What do you mean?"

"There are two doors into the kitchen—one from the hallway and one from the fellowship hall."

"Ah. We could pretend one of them is jammed or something."

"Leave it with me. I'll figure it out."

"Thanks. There's one more thing. We need to keep Suzanne completely away from the church from now through the end of the dinner."

He leaned back in his chair and laughed. "Good luck with that."

"You underestimate me, my friend."

Greg winced at the "friend" but didn't say anything.

"I have a plan for Suzanne, too. Since the visitation is tonight, nobody will be able to work on the float. My idea is for you to round up a bunch of the youth group to go over there now and spend the rest of the day. Suzanne won't want to leave them there without her supervision, so she'll be forced to stay with them. You could even offer to provide pizzas for dinner, to keep the kids there that long. I'll pay for it."

"I appreciate that offer, but I'll take it out of the youth budget. And I'll talk to Suzanne and start calling the kids."

"Get the kids ready to head over there before you talk to Suzanne. That way she can't weasel her way out of it. But make sure to tell the kids they need to leave at 6:00, so Suzanne will be able to come to the visitation."

"Got it." He moved to his desk and began making phone calls.

I left the office in search of Veronica. Suzanne was playing the piano in the choir room again, so I tiptoed past and then found Veronica in the fellowship hall. She had roped her husband into helping make silk flower arrangements for the tables. I smiled at the sight.

She spotted me in the doorway and waved me over. "Come help us."

"I'm enjoying this immensely," Pastor Coker said to me. "Who knew I'd like flower arranging? Gets the creative juices flowing, my dear."

"That's great!" But not so great for getting him to leave so I could talk to his wife. I'd need to get her out of the room instead.

"I'm happy to help," I said, "but first, I need Mrs. Coker's advice on something."

"Well, I'm happy to give it," she said. "What do you need?"

"Uh, it's about something ... personal."

"Oh!" Pastor Coker said. "I can go." He set down a silk rose he'd been attempting to place.

"No, no, you stay here," I said, "since you're enjoying it so much. We'll step out for a minute."

I led Veronica out of the room and into a Sunday school classroom across the hall. I closed the door but didn't turn on the lights. Veronica took a seat in the only adult-sized chair in the room. Instead of trying to sit on one of the child-sized chairs in my skirt, I perched on the edge of a table. Veronica raised an eyebrow at me but didn't say anything.

"Did you get time to talk to your husband about the investigation?"

"No, I was afraid someone might come in on us while I was telling him. I'll do it when we go home for lunch."

"You might not want to do it yet. But again, that's your decision."

I told her the plan for the dinner.

"That means once the first dish arrives," I said, "at least one of us will need to be in the kitchen at all times. We'll also need to rearrange the fellowship hall a little, to remove the serving tables. And we need a reasonable explanation for why we're serving differently than usual."

"We can tell people it was my idea—something new we're trying. They won't question me. Well, Suzanne might, especially since this wasn't the plan an hour ago when we started setting up the room."

"Greg is going to keep her out of the way." I explained the

situation.

"Excellent plan." She stood. "You'd better get into the kitchen, and Harold and I will finish the decorations. After he's gone back to the office, we'll rearrange. No need for him to ask questions."

"You're not going to tell him what's happening?" I followed her to the door.

"No way. If he thinks someone might be poisoned at the dinner, he'll be as nervous as a cat. Best he stays in the dark for now." She paused before opening the door. "But we'd better pray about this whole thing. I have to say, it's making me a little nervous, too."

I nodded, and she bowed her head and said a precise but succinct prayer. When she finished, I had no doubt nobody would die at the church that evening.

We stepped into the hallway and were greeted by shouting from the direction of the choir room.

SEVENTEEN

"WHAT'S SUZANNE WORKED UP ABOUT?" Veronica marched down the hall toward the choir room.

Pastor Coker ambled out of the fellowship hall to see what the ruckus was about. "Ah, Suzanne. Looks like Veronica's taking care of it." He turned and disappeared back into the room.

I followed Veronica, thankful she was there. If anybody could get Suzanne to do something she didn't want to do, it was our pastor's wife.

Veronica stopped in the doorway of the choir room and put her hands on her hips. "Suzanne LaHaye, is that any way to speak to a pastor? Or anyone, for that matter? You are a Christian woman. Get ahold of yourself."

I peeked around Veronica. Suzanne was breathing heavily, and her face was beet red. Her finger pointed at Greg, who stood a few feet from her with a deer-in-the-headlights look. His eyes darted back and forth between Suzanne and Veronica, but the rest of his body was rigid.

"He," Suzanne jabbed her finger toward Greg, "told the entire youth group to go to my house today to work on the float. I need to be here, not there. He had no right!"

Veronica slowly walked toward Suzanne, and I skirted around her to stand in solidarity with Greg.

"I'm sure *Pastor* Greg is only trying to help," Veronica said. "You don't want to put off the work until tomorrow night. What if it doesn't get finished? Today is the perfect time to do it. You don't need to be here. You've played those songs beautifully thousands of times. There's no reason to practice any more. And we'll make sure everything is covered for the dinner." She placed her hand on Suzanne's shoulder. "You go spend some time with those youngsters. They look up to you, you know."

Veronica was laying it on thick, but I wasn't about to interrupt her. Suzanne dropped her finger and didn't shake Veronica's hand off, which were both positive signs.

"Take a deep breath ..."

Suzanne breathed in and out deeply.

"... and let yourself think clearly for a moment."

Suzanne sank down onto the piano bench and put her head in her hands. After a few seconds, she raised her head and focused on Greg, who was finally starting to relax. "I'm sorry." She picked at a fingernail. "I just want to be here to help Georgia in any way I can. It's terrible, what's happened."

I squeezed onto the bench next to Suzanne and put an arm around her. "Yes, it is terrible, and you've already done so much to help. Now go take care of those kids. I'm sure Greg will make sure they leave in time for you to come pay your respects tonight."

"Definitely," he said. "I'll even make sure they get fed."

Veronica clapped her hands together. "It's all set, then. You head on home, Suzanne. We'll make sure to call you if you're needed here."

Veronica helped Suzanne to her feet and escorted her out of the room.

I scooted over to the middle of the piano bench. "I am *so* sorry about that."

Greg gave me a shaky grin. "You owe me one for that. I thought she was going to have an aneurysm right here in front of me."

"I'll make it up to you somehow. I'll make all this mess up to you. Just as soon as this murder is solved."

"I'm going to hold you to it."

I hoped he didn't get the wrong idea about what I was saying, but I couldn't deal with that at the moment, so I stood. "I'd better go set up shop in the kitchen."

"You want me to move a few chairs in there for you ladies?"

"That would be awesome."

I took off for the office to grab some paper and a pen to write down any phone messages. I also grabbed my purse so I'd have my suspect notebook on hand. Then I told Pastor Coker I'd be in the kitchen most of the afternoon getting ready for the dinner. He was working on his funeral message, so he didn't have the mental focus to question why it would take me five hours to get ready. I felt bad for not telling him what was going on, but I wasn't going to go against Veronica's decision.

Greg and I met in the hall as he returned from the kitchen. "Got you all set up in there. Also, I think I've figured out a plan to block one of the doors. I put a table in front of the door from the fellowship hall into the kitchen. You can use it for drinks, and you can restock it through the door when needed."

"Excellent plan. Thanks!"

We started to head our separate ways when I said, "Hold up a minute." I spun back around, almost falling in the process. I caught myself on the wall.

Greg saw my mishap and immediately rushed over to steady me. "You okay there? What is it?"

I stood up straight, and he let go of me.

"I was thinking we should make sure all the doors are locked. We'll put signs on all of them saying to bring any food to the door down near the kitchen and knock loudly."

"Great idea," he said. "If you make the signs, I'll put them up and make sure all the doors are locked."

"I'll use the supplies in the youth room. When I'm done, I'll bring the signs to the office." I paused. "No, wait a minute. I don't want Pastor Coker to wonder what we're doing. Come grab them from the youth room in about five minutes?"

"Will do."

———

AN HOUR LATER, the signs were on the doors, Trixie had arrived, and we had received a bowl of fruit cocktail and a platter of oatmeal raisin cookies, both from people in no way connected to anyone at the reunion. The two ladies asked why the doors were locked, and I said we'd been told to be careful after Aidan's death, and even more so now.

Brrrring!

I answered the phone on the kitchen wall. "First Comm. This is Beckett. How may I help you?"

"Hey there."

My heart rate increased. I turned to Trixie, pointed at the phone with my other hand, and mouthed, "Mitchell."

She whispered, "Well, talk to him!"

"Hey." I tried to sound nonchalant. "What's up?"

"I ran back to The Osh for a minute and wanted to call. I'm glad you answered."

"What if someone else had picked up?"

"I would have hung up."

"Anything new I need to know?"

"Can't really say. You got everything set up at the church for the dinner?"

"Yes, Trixie's here with me. Oh, and I told Greg about the dinner plans, because I needed his help. He won't tell a soul, though."

"Greg the youth leader guy?"

"Yes."

"Hmm."

Mitchell saw Greg as a rival, though he needn't.

"He can be trusted. Anyway, all the outside doors are locked, and we're only letting people bring food to the door near the kitchen. Nothing suspicious yet."

"Good. Darren and I are planning to be there tonight."

"For the dinner?"

"Yes, and the visitation. We'll both be in plainclothes, and we'll be armed. It's standard during a murder investigation."

"Oh. I guess I didn't notice any officers on duty at Aidan's visitation."

"That's kind of the point."

We were both silent for a moment.

"You doing okay?" he asked. "Did you sleep all right?"

"I slept fine. I don't like that someone was in my house without my permission, though. Last night threw me for a loop."

"There were a couple of very nice moments last night, though, if I recall."

"Mmhm." My face heated, and I turned away from Trixie. I was glad Mitchell couldn't see me.

"You're blushing, aren't you?"

"Yes. I can't imagine why."

He chuckled.

"There's nothing new you can tell me?" I asked. "I know you searched the Stouffer barn and the shed at Marty and Kyle's place."

"How'd you hear that?"

"Veronica saw the police cars. Did you find anything? If you did, I think it would be best for me to know, considering the situation we're in with the dinner."

"Okay, you've talked me into it."

"That wasn't too hard."

"I am rather concerned about you, after all."

167

I smiled. "Thanks. Now what do you know?"

I waved Trixie over and tilted the phone so she could hear him.

"We found old pesticides containing high concentrations of cyanide at both places," he said. "But we also found some in Jeff Jenkins' garage, in the shed in Billy's parents' backyard, and at the fertilizer plant. And Frank told us there's some in his horse barn."

"That means any of your suspects would have access to it."

"Yes. We got fingerprints off all the containers, but that won't tell us anything, unless we find some that shouldn't be there— like from someone who doesn't live at those places. And the person probably wore gloves to handle it anyway. I would, with something that toxic, even if I didn't have bad intentions. We also don't have everyone's prints on file yet, but we're working on it."

"Hmm. Doesn't sound like any of that is going to help."

"Probably not. Darren told you to set aside any food from people at the reunion, right?"

"Yes."

"Don't dump it out. We'll want to get it tested, so make sure you label everything. And wash your hands well after touching any of it."

"Yes, sir. Anything else we need to know?"

"I don't think so."

"When you're here tonight, do we all ignore you and pretend we don't know why you're here? Or can we talk? How does this work?"

"Well, you definitely can't kiss me."

Trixie grinned and stepped away from the phone. After hesitating a second, she walked into the hall, closing the door behind her.

He continued, "Unless there's a janitor's closet handy?"

I burst out laughing. "We should probably avoid all closets tonight."

"That's likely for the best ... for now. Especially since I'll be on duty, which also means we probably shouldn't talk or even be close to each other if we can help it. I don't need any distractions."

"I'm a distraction now, am I?"

"More than you know." He paused. "Stop your blushing."

I giggled.

"I need to get back to the station," he said. "I'll see you in a few hours."

"See you then."

I hung up and smiled at the empty kitchen for a few moments before crossing the room to open the door. Trixie was sitting on the hall floor near the outside door with a serving bowl covered in foil next to her. She jumped up when she saw me and nudged the bowl with her foot.

"Cheryl brought this."

"What is it?"

"I don't know. I'm afraid to touch it again. I really need to wash my hands."

"Leave it to me." I went back into the kitchen and grabbed some hand towels. I used them to pick up the bowl and transport it to the pantry. Then I nudged Trixie away from the sink, where she'd been washing her hands longer than necessary, and soaped up my own hands.

"You think I should call the station and tell the guys about this?" I rinsed the soap off and dried my hands. "They might want to go ahead and pick it up for testing."

"Won't hurt to ask."

Pounding sounded on the outside door. I peeked down the hallway, where my aunt stood on the other side of the glass door holding two paper bags. I rushed down to let her in and take one of the bags.

"Good idea to keep the doors all locked." She followed me down the hall. "I got us some lunch from The Check."

"Thanks. We got our first suspicious dish from Cheryl. We were getting ready to call Darren to see if he wants to pick it up."

"I'll do it. It'll be less suspicious if I call there than you, since they don't want everyone at the station to know what's going on."

"Great idea."

She made the call, and Darren said he'd come pick it up in a minute, but we shouldn't touch it again. We waited for him near the outside door, so he wouldn't have to stand outside any longer than necessary.

"Barbara usually answers calls to the station, but one of the officers did instead," Aunt Star said. "I wonder if that's related to her daughter being a suspect."

"I still don't understand what Cheryl's motive would be," I said.

Darren's pickup pulled up near the door, and he hopped out, carrying a cardboard box with a lid. Trixie held the door open for him.

I said, "Already in plainclothes, I see."

"And smooth move driving your truck instead of a police car." Trixie gave him a thumbs-up.

Darren gave us an amused smile. "I appreciate the approval of my methods. Lead me to the food."

We all trooped up the hallway, and I led him through the kitchen and into the pantry. He pulled some rubber gloves out of the box, put them on, moved the dish into the box, and covered it with the lid.

As he peeled the gloves back off, he asked, "How did Cheryl act? Anything off about her?"

Trixie responded, "She seemed a little put out that I wouldn't let her come in. She also questioned why I was here, since I don't go to church here. Not that she does either, but her parents-in-law do. I told her Beckett asked me to help, and the church asked us to be cautious. I tried not to make a big deal about it."

"All right. Let me know if you get any more food we need to test. It's best for Starla to call, since she often calls the station anyway."

"That's why I called this time," my aunt said.

"Great. Call the minute anything else comes in. I'll be sending Officer Park to the lab in Jefferson City with this one sometime in the next hour, so hopefully we can get a result back before the end of the day. Would be nice to not have him make another trip later, both for the time it would take and because others will wonder why he's gone again."

"You must trust Officer Park, or you wouldn't have told him about this," Aunt Star said. "You don't think he's your leak?"

"He's new and not from around here, so he wouldn't have any allegiances to anyone that I know of. And we needed to trust somebody, because Detective Crowe and I need to both stay in town all day."

"Speaking of trusting people," I said, "I told Greg. Otherwise, I wouldn't have been able to keep Suzanne away. He's also going to help keep people out of the kitchen during the dinner."

"Good to know." He started toward the door. "I'd better get out of here before somebody sees me."

When he left, I said, "From now on, I should probably be the only one to go to the door, so we don't get more questions about why non-church-members are here, but church members aren't allowed in."

"They'll see our cars, though," Aunt Star said.

"Why don't you go move them to the street instead of the parking lot?"

They took turns leaving and moving their cars.

When we were all settled back in, we ate our lunch and I told Aunt Star what Mitchell said about finding cyanide.

"Why did they search Jeff Jenkins' garage?" she asked.

"He didn't say."

"Did they search anywhere and *not* find cyanide?"

"Good question," Trixie said. "He didn't say that either."

We ate in silence for a few minutes. I was thankful I wasn't alone after the events of the previous evening. I also would have been very bored waiting in the kitchen by myself all afternoon. There weren't even any windows in the room, so it was extremely quiet. We all jumped in our seats when someone pounded on the outside door.

EIGHTEEN

SINCE ANSWERING THE DOOR had become my job, I got up. Donna Jenkins stood on the other side of the door holding an orange Tupperware bowl. I opened the door, and she started to step inside, but I stopped her.

"Sorry," I said, "but we're being cautious around here these days."

"What? You think I'm a murderer?" She laughed and handed me the bowl.

I took it and held it gingerly. "No, but I can't really pick and choose who I want to let in. If I don't let *anyone* in, then nobody can be offended, right?"

"I guess that makes sense. I better not hear you let Karla in. Or Anita." She laughed. "I'm kidding." She pointed at the bowl. "I brought some of my homemade applesauce."

"Sounds delicious. Thanks! Will I see you at the visitation tonight?"

"Of course. Got some important business to take care of first, but then I'll be back."

"Great. See you then."

I took the bowl back to the kitchen. "Call Darren," I told Aunt Star. "This is from Donna Jenkins."

She hopped up and made the call while I washed my hands. Their conversation was brief, and she ended it with, "See you soon." She hung up and said, "Officer Park was on his way out the door. Caught him just in time."

A few minutes later, I let Darren in again.

"Donna doesn't go to church here, does she?" he asked.

"No," I said, "she and Jeff used to go to the Methodist church, but I don't think either of them go anywhere since the divorce. None of their parents attend here, either."

Darren wasted no time packing up the bowl in his box and heading out again.

He hadn't been gone a minute when Greg appeared with the boombox from the youth room. "Thought you ladies might want to listen to some music while you wait." He set the music player on the counter and plugged it in.

"Everything good?" he asked as he extended the antenna.

"All going according to plan," I replied. If Greg hadn't seen Darren either time, I didn't feel the need to fill him in on the details.

He made small talk for a few minutes and then left to check on how things were going at Suzanne's.

I turned the radio on but left the volume low enough so we could still hear anyone at the door. Trixie sang along to "Centerfield" as I pulled my suspect notebook out of my purse.

"Ladies, let's solve this murder," I said.

"You weren't planning to wait for me?" Veronica stood in the doorway.

"Hi! I didn't know if you'd be able to join us or not."

"Let me get you a chair." Trixie went to grab one from the fellowship hall.

"Does Pastor Coker suspect anything strange is going on?"

"He's completely oblivious."

We filled her in on what we'd learned since I'd last seen her.

"So as of last night, the police were looking at Kyle, Karla, and Cheryl. But we eliminated Karla, because she couldn't have broken into our house."

"That leaves us with Kyle and Cheryl," Trixie said.

"I vote for Kyle," Aunt Star said. "He has a decent motive, and the police found cyanide at his house and his work."

"He was also at the reunion with plenty of time to do the deed," Trixie said. "And he made sure he was occupied at the time Paula's body was discovered."

Pounding sounded from the hallway.

"I'll take care of it." Veronica stepped out of the room.

She returned a minute later with a roasting pan and set it on the counter. "Ham. From Wynette Smith. Any connections to the murder?"

We all thought for a few seconds and then shook our heads. Veronica turned the oven on low and slid the pan inside.

I said to her, "How are we going to keep all the church ladies from trying to join us here in the kitchen during the dinner, like they usually do? Greg said he would help keep people out of here, but after what happened with Suzanne, I don't want to put him through something like that again."

"I've called around and told them we put together some strict rules regarding the dinner due to the killer still running loose. They won't give us any trouble."

"Good." I wondered what exactly she'd said. Some of the ladies could be persistent—even mouthy—but Veronica could hold her own with anybody. "Is that somebody knocking?"

We craned our necks toward the door. All we could hear was the radio for a moment, but then light tapping sounded. Veronica headed back out. The most recent arrival was a baking dish of scalloped potatoes, provided by another person not connected to Paula.

"Back to the investigation," I said, "what about Donna? The police haven't mentioned her at all, but she was in the pictures talking to Paula right before she died, and she teaches chemistry. And why did she bring food today? How did she even know to bring anything?"

"It would be easy enough for anyone in town to find out about the dinner," Aunt Star said.

"Donna had the means and opportunity," Trixie said, "but what's her motive?"

More knocking interrupted our conversation. For the next hour, we received a steady stream of food deliveries and phone calls, so we didn't get back to our suspect list. Thankfully we didn't get any more food from potential suspects or their families.

Aunt Star and Veronica both left to change into their funeral visitation attire, while Trixie stayed to keep me company and get the fellowship hall set up the way we wanted it.

"Let's go back to Donna," Trixie said as we rolled silverware into napkins and the Nitty Gritty Dirt Band sang "Modern Day Romance" in the background. "Why would she kill Paula?"

"I don't know." I grabbed a fork, spoon, and knife and placed them on a napkin. "It sounds like they hadn't even talked to each other in years."

"That's what Donna says, but maybe that's not true."

"Maybe. But there's no reason to think she had any motive to hurt Paula."

Another knock on the door sent me back into the hall. Aunt Star had gotten herself ready in record time and was carrying one of my black dresses and a duffel bag.

She handed me the hanger. "I picked out your sexiest black dress, considering Mitchell will be here."

"Not sure that's the best idea for church or a funeral," I said, "but I do appreciate the gesture." Not that my sexiest dress was anywhere near inappropriate. It was cut down lower in the front than my others, but still well above even the dress Aunt Star was wearing, and she always looked classy.

When we reached the kitchen, I took the bag from her and slipped into the Sunday school room across the hall. Without turning on the lights, I headed to the tiny bathroom connecting the room to the next one. The sink and toilet were at toddler height, but that also meant the mirror over the sink nearly doubled as a full-length mirror.

While I changed out of my colorful shirt and skirt and wriggled into a fresh pair of pantyhose and the tight black dress, I pondered the suspects yet again. I agreed with Aunt Star that Kyle had the best motive of anyone who hadn't been clearly eliminated, though I didn't know the reason the police decided Billy didn't do it. I decided to trust Mitchell and Darren's investigative work and believe that Billy was not the killer, which was a huge relief.

It was difficult to believe Kyle could kill someone, though—especially a woman. The man was an obnoxious flirt, but he'd never had much of a temper, at least not when we were kids. He had been devastated when Karla dumped him and left town, though. I wondered if Paula had anything to do with that. I couldn't imagine what, but I hadn't been close to her, Karla, or Kyle during our senior year, so I couldn't discount it.

I touched up my makeup, and my thoughts turned to Mitchell. I hoped he'd wear a suit to the dinner and visitation. Though I'd never seen him in anything as casual as a T-shirt and jeans, I'd also never seen him fully decked out in a suit. I looked forward to the experience.

I packed my duffel bag and made my way back through the classroom, but the sky had darkened while I was in the bathroom, and I tripped over a miniature chair that wasn't completely pushed under the table. I fell against a metal storage cabinet and slid to the floor. Moments later, Trixie and Aunt Star rushed into the room.

"Becks, what happened?" My aunt knelt next to me.

"I tripped on a chair. I think I'm okay."

Trixie held out a hand. I grabbed it, and she slowly pulled me up, with Aunt Star's assistance.

I rotated my shoulder a few times and then rubbed it. "That's going to leave a mark, but I'll be all right."

"You sure?"

"Yep."

"Your zipper has come undone," Trixie said.

"It never was done. I couldn't quite reach it to zip it all the way up. Can you help me out?" I held my hair up while Trixie pulled up the zipper.

I stumbled a bit when I started to walk, and Trixie caught me. "You sure you're all right?"

"My legs are fine. Well, as fine as they ever are." She held onto me the rest of the way to the kitchen and directed me into a chair.

"Sit there for a few minutes. We can handle this."

The two began setting some of the non-perishable food out on the counter. I checked my watch to find it was 3:50.

"Trix, you'd better run home and change."

"I was waiting until you got back out here, so Starla wouldn't be on her own. But I'll head out now."

Veronica arrived soon after Trixie left. She gave my dress a once-over and pursed her lips, but she didn't comment on the neckline, for which I was grateful.

She made for the refrigerator and started pulling out dishes. I uncovered them and added serving spoons as needed. Aunt Star placed them on the counter in easy reach for us but not for those going through the line on the other side.

While the two of them prepared the hot foods, I placed some giant plastic bowls on the drinks table, filled them with soda cans, and covered them with ice. I set a stack of Styrofoam cups by the sink in case anyone requested water.

Greg came in at 4:20, with Trixie on his heels. He also gave me a once-over and formed his lips like he was going to whistle. Thankfully he thought better of it.

At 4:25, a knock sounded on the outside door. We all looked at each other. I peeked down the hallway and saw Billy and other family members on the other side of the door.

"Ready?" I asked.

"We can't leave the family standing in the heat," Veronica said. "I'll let them in, and I'll smooth things over with Georgia about the different plan. I'll probably spend most of my time with the family in the fellowship hall, unless one of you asks me for help here in the kitchen."

"And I'll stand guard out in the hallway," Greg said.

Veronica looked toward the ceiling, put her hand on her heart, said, "God, help us," and marched out.

Greg followed and closed the door behind him.

People started trickling into the fellowship hall. Billy waved at us, and his twin sisters both came over to say hi. Darren entered, shook Billy's hand, and acknowledged our presence with a slight nod. His eyes lingered on Aunt Star for a moment before he grabbed a soda and took a seat at a table in the far corner where he could observe the entire room. One of Billy's sisters—the single one—soon joined him.

I nudged Aunt Star, who said, "I have eyes, but I'm not worried. Darren would never consider even flirting with another woman."

"You snagged yourself a good one there, Star," Trixie said.

"I know it." Aunt Star smiled at the man in question across the room.

"Just don't do anything to ruin it," I said.

"Now why would you go and say a thing like that?" my aunt demanded.

"That was uncalled for, Beck," Trixie said.

I put my hand on Aunt Star's arm, and she didn't pull away. "It was. I'm sorry. I don't know what I was thinking."

She briefly put her hand over mine. "Apology accepted.

We're all a little jumpy right now."

Veronica clapped her hands a few times and announced, "If everyone can quiet down, the pastor will say a prayer, and we will eat." When the talking died down, she continued, "We're doing things a little differently tonight, under these strange circumstances, so please be patient with us." The tone of her voice left no room for questioning. "These lovely ladies," she swept her hand toward us, "will fill your plates for you. Let them know what you want, and they'll take care of everything."

Pastor Coker prayed, and when I raised my head afterward, Mitchell had slipped into the room. He was, indeed, wearing a suit. I watched him make eye contact with Darren and then do a quick visual sweep of the room. When he was finished, his eyes sought mine. To my dismay, my face started heating when we locked eyes. He struggled not to grin. He put his hand over his mouth, as if covering a cough, but I knew better.

"Time to focus on the food, ladies, not the officers of the law," Trixie murmured as she moved to the counter, where a line was beginning to form.

The process went much more smoothly than I had anticipated as everyone made their way through the line. By the time we filled everyone's plate, my stomach was rumbling, but I wasn't about to let Darren see me eating any of the food.

"I brought some sandwiches and chips if you're hungry," Trixie said in a low voice. "They're in a bag in the pantry."

"We'd better eat in there," I said, "or people will ask why we're not eating this food." I nodded at the counter.

"You go ahead," Aunt Star said, "I heard your stomach growling."

I slipped into the pantry and scarfed down a ham sandwich and a handful of chips. When I returned, Trixie said, "Billy was looking for you. Go on out there and talk to him if you want. We're fine in here."

I opened the kitchen door without paying attention to what I was doing and ran into Greg, who was standing directly outside the door. He spun around and grabbed me by the waist before I could fall to the floor. At the same moment, Mitchell came out the fellowship hall door ten feet away.

NINETEEN

GREG AND I WERE positioned so I could see Mitchell but Greg couldn't. Mitchell's gaze darted from my eyes to Greg's hands at my waist and back up to my eyes. He stood stock still and his face was devoid of expression. I stepped backward, out of Greg's grasp.

"Thanks for catching me," I said to Greg, only momentarily breaking eye contact with Mitchell. "Glad I didn't hit the ground twice in one day."

Understanding flickered in Mitchell's eyes, and he rushed toward us.

"What's this about hitting the ground?"

Greg moved to the side and watched warily as Mitchell took hold of my wrists and checked me over from head to toe, but not in a way that would make me blush. For one thing, he was frowning. For another, he reminded me of my mother when I hurt myself as a child.

"I fell earlier," I explained. "Well, I tripped, fell against a cabinet, and slid to the floor. You know me!" I said brightly.

I could see the struggle in Mitchell's face. He wanted to wrap me in his arms, and there was nothing I wanted more, but this wasn't the time or place. I briefly closed my eyes and then stepped backward again, out of his hold.

"I'm fine. Don't worry."

He nodded. "Why are you here in the hall? I saw you open the door, and I wanted to make sure nobody was loitering out here." He paused. "Except Greg, of course." He turned to where Greg was leaned against the wall a few feet away with his hands in his pockets. "Thanks for helping us out, man."

"Glad to help."

I thought Greg might walk away and give us some privacy, but I thought wrong.

"Trixie said Billy was asking for me. I was heading to the fellowship hall to talk to him."

"You think that's a good idea?" Mitchell spoke quietly, but not enough for Greg to not be able to hear him.

I narrowed my eyes at him. "I think it's a perfectly fine idea for me to go talk to my friend, thank you very much." Billy was no longer a suspect, so what was Mitchell's problem with it? And I didn't appreciate him questioning me in front of Greg.

His eyes widened. "Sorry. I shouldn't have questioned your decision."

My tone softened, "We're all a little tightly wound tonight. You're forgiven. And I'm sorry for snapping back at you. Now, can I ...?" I nodded toward the fellowship hall door, but he was standing in my way.

"Oh, right."

Mitchell moved aside and then followed me into the room. I was afraid he was going to trail me all the way to Billy, but he stationed himself next to the window into the kitchen and said something to Aunt Star and Trixie.

Billy spotted me coming toward him and came to meet me.

"Is there somewhere we can talk? Alone?"

It was one thing to talk to him. It was another thing to be alone with him. But if he wasn't a suspect, I figured it would be safe enough. And anyway, I wanted to know what he had to say. I turned to look at Mitchell, who didn't even try to pretend he wasn't watching us.

"Need permission from your boyfriend before you say yes?" Billy asked.

My attention snapped back to him. His mild expression belied the snark in his tone.

"No," I snapped back. "I can do what I want."

"Well, do you want to talk to me?"

I cocked my head and assessed him. Though he was acting belligerent, I could see the pain in his eyes, and my heart went out to him. The man had just lost his wife.

I sighed. "Yes. Come on." I shot Mitchell a pleading look as I walked toward the door.

Billy matched my stride. "He going to follow us?"

"He'd better not," I lied. I had no doubt he would, but Billy might never know it.

Once we were in the hall, I said, "We can talk in the sanctuary." I stared at Greg while I said it, and he nodded from his post by the kitchen door.

Billy didn't say anything until we were almost to the sanctuary. "What's up with that guy in the hall? He creeped me out a little bit."

"Greg? He's a good guy but can be intense sometimes." Greg wouldn't know intense if it hit him in the head. I was racking up quite the list of lies I would feel guilty about later.

We entered the sanctuary through the open double doors at the back. Mr. Cooper was at the front of the room with the local florist, setting the arrangements on tiered stands and on the casket, which was thankfully closed. Usually, the early evening light would be streaming in through the west-facing stained-glass windows, but a storm was rolling in, so the overhead lights were on.

My attention snapped to the funeral director and florist. I guessed Pastor Coker had let them in, because I had completely forgotten about anything other than what was happening in the kitchen that afternoon. I also should have considered the fact that the casket would have arrived and the room might not be the best place to bring Billy.

I didn't have the patience or the energy to go elsewhere, so I slipped into the back pew, and Billy slid in next to me after taking off his suit coat and draping it over the back of the pew in front of me. He angled his long legs in my direction and laid his arm along the back of the pew. I scooted a little farther away from him, but not enough to make a statement.

"All those empty rooms, and you chose the one with people in it?" he asked.

"Hey, do you want to talk or not? They're not paying any attention to us, and they can't hear us anyway. Speak softly and we'll be fine."

"Okay."

A slight movement through the crack between the open sanctuary door and the doorjamb caught my eye. I prayed it was Mitchell, and that he could hear us. But with Billy facing away from him and talking softly—on my suggestion—I wasn't sure.

"What do you need to tell me?" I prompted.

"That I didn't do it," he said in a hushed but vehement tone. "I didn't kill Paula."

The room briefly lit up, and I turned toward the windows. A few seconds later, thunder boomed, and my body jerked, even though I knew it was coming.

I turned back to Billy. "I know you didn't."

His eyes widened. "You do?"

"Yes." I had hoped I believed it before, but now I truly knew I did.

He let out a long breath, and his body visibly relaxed. "You don't know what that means to me. When I didn't hear from you again after you stopped by Saturday night, I thought you believed the worst of me. It wasn't a great feeling to know the police, probably some of our classmates, and maybe even Paula's family suspected me. But thinking that *you* considered I could be a murderer? That crushed me." He turned his face away from me.

"Even Kyle stopped by yesterday."

I wanted to reach out and comfort him, but with Mitchell potentially watching, I knew I couldn't—at least not if I didn't want him crashing the conversation.

"Billy," I said, but he kept his face averted. I lightly and quickly touched his arm. "Billy, look at me."

He turned, and a single tear ran down his cheek.

"I'm sorry I didn't call or stop by, but I've been busy."

He started to protest, but I held a hand up to stop him.

"I've been busy trying to figure out who did kill Paula."

"What? But that's—"

"The police's job? I know. I've been told. By them. Many times."

I grinned at him, and he gave me a weak smile in return.

"Becky, back in high school ... I'm sorry for what I did. I don't think I ever told you that."

"No, you didn't."

"I loved you, you know. More than I ever—"

I shot my hand out and covered his mouth before he could say what I thought he was going to say. "Don't say it." I jerked my head toward the casket. "Especially not here."

He nodded, and I dropped my hand. I was surprised Mitchell hadn't rushed in and tackled Billy. He must not have seen my movement, because he would have misinterpreted it.

"I did love her, though. Things ... it was bad after Zachary came."

"I know. Georgia told me."

"Georgia doesn't know the truth of it. Paula didn't withdraw from everyone, like her mother believes. Well, she did a bit. But mostly people stopped calling and coming around because Paula became condescending and spiteful. I heard her talking to Donna on the phone one time after her divorce, and some of the things she said were downright nasty. I couldn't believe my ears."

Lightning flashed again, followed more closely by thunder than the last time.

"That is surprising, but Donna has an extremely thick skin."

"I don't think you understand," Billy said. "Did you know Donna can't have kids?"

My hand flew to my heart. "What? No!"

"She had an emergency hysterectomy about four years ago. She was devastated."

"Oh, Donna." Tears filled my eyes.

"Paula was sad for her, too. Or at least she was before Zachary. That's how I think about our life now—before Zachary and after Zachary." He took a deep breath. "Paula lorded it over Donna that she had a baby and Donna never would. She also bragged about how strong our marriage was, when Donna's had recently broken up. It was terrible. And it was a lie. Our marriage was a disaster."

Rain pounded on the roof. We both looked up in silence for a moment.

"I'm so sorry, Billy."

"That's not to say Donna and Jeff's marriage wasn't a disaster, too. The man tended to fawn over Paula when we were all together. He never crossed a line, but he made me uncomfortable at times, though Paula never seemed to mind. I only put up with him because Paula and Donna were friends. Can't say I wasn't glad when they split up. Donna deserves better than Jeff."

"Hey, now," I said playfully, and lightly punched his arm. "You're talking about my old boyfriend."

Anger flashed in Billy's eyes. "I *hated* that you dated him. You definitely deserved much better than Jeff Jenkins. But there wasn't a whole lot I could do about it, was there?"

"No, you gave up your right to have any opinion about who I spent my time with."

"I was pretty dumb, wasn't I?"

I gave him a sad smile. "Don't be too hard on yourself. After all, I chose to date Jeff."

Billy snorted, and I giggled.

We sat in companionable silence for a while, and I thought about everything Billy had just said. I turned to him. "Did you say Kyle came to see you yesterday?"

"Yeah, why?"

"Never mind why. What time?"

"He stopped by on his way home from work, so I guess a little after five o'clock."

"How long did he stay?"

"Quite a while. I was glad he came by, but he more than wore out his welcome. You know how he is. But I didn't have the heart to kick him out. Thankfully Cheryl called while he was there, so I got a break from him for about a half hour."

"Hold up. What time did Cheryl call?"

"Right at 5:45. I remember looking at the clock when Mom asked me to come to the phone. My poor dad was itching to get away from Kyle by the time I got off with Cheryl. Kyle finally left when we were ready to eat dinner. Mom sent him on his way before he could invite himself."

"What time do you think that was?"

"Maybe 6:30?"

I sat up straight. If Kyle was at the Arbuckle house from 5:00 until 6:30, he couldn't have broken into our house. And if Cheryl was on the phone most of the time Aunt Star and I were at Jazzercise, it couldn't have been her, either. But Billy had provided a perfect motive for the real killer.

"What?" Billy grabbed my shoulder. "What have you figured out?"

"I'll tell you later. I need to talk to Mitchell." I pushed to my feet and nearly tripped over Billy's legs in my haste to exit the pew. He grabbed my waist to keep me upright, and I rushed out the door.

TWENTY

I EXPECTED TO FIND Mitchell lurking in the foyer, but the space was empty. Had he heard us and figured it out before I did?

Thunder crashed again as I ran down the hall as fast as I could in my pumps and with my bad leg. I blew right past Greg and skidded to a halt in the doorway of the fellowship hall but managed to stay on my feet. I scanned the room, but I found neither Mitchell nor Darren. I yelped when someone tapped me on the shoulder.

"Sorry," Greg said from behind me. "Didn't mean to startle you."

I turned to him. "What?" I said breathlessly.

"Your, uh, detective guy and Officer Turley just left."

I figured this wasn't the time to correct him on Darren's rank or Mitchell's name.

"Where'd they go?"

"They didn't tell me, but Officer Turley went into the kitchen at one point, so the other women might know."

"Great."

I pushed past him and scurried down the hall and into the kitchen. I didn't mean to slam the door in his face, but that's what happened. I had no time to make apologies, though.

"What's happening? Where did the guys go?"

"They didn't say." Aunt Star's hands were clasped together tightly.

I pointed at her hands. "Why are you doing that?"

"What?" She looked down. "Oh. Might be a little anxious."

"Why? What in the world is going on?" I hissed. I wanted to shout, but I didn't want to cause a scene, since we could be seen from the fellowship hall.

Trixie opened the pantry door. "Get in here, and I'll tell you what we know."

Aunt Star and Veronica both joined us in the cramped space.

"You left with Billy, and Mitchell followed you. Greg told him where to go. Good job on leaving that clue, by the way. Greg told us what you did."

"Thanks."

"Then the phone rang," Veronica said impatiently. "It was Frank, calling from the police station. He said he needed to talk to Detective Crowe or Darren immediately. Detective Crowe was keeping an eye on you, so we got Darren. By the way, I need to know what's going on between you and this detective."

"In due time. Please finish the story! Hurry!"

Aunt Star said, "We couldn't make heads nor tails of what Darren was saying to Frank. He didn't say much other than police speak. The infuriating man didn't give us a thing to work with!"

I grabbed her hands. "You need to take a deep breath. And somebody needs to finish this dang story!"

"Okay, you need to take a breath, too," Trixie said. "Darren then rushed out to look for Mitchell, and Greg directed him to the sanctuary. A minute later they came flying back down the hallway and out the door into the storm."

"You don't know where they were going?" I asked.

"No idea. Now why are you so worked up?" Veronica asked.

"Because I know who the killer is!"

"Well, why didn't you lead with that?" Aunt Star asked. "Who is it?"

"Donna."

Their jaws dropped.

"But why?" Aunt Star asked. "What did she have against Paula?"

"No time to explain. We've got to go!"

"Go where? And do what?"

"When Donna was here earlier, she said she had some important business to take care of, but she'd be back for the visitation. What if she was planning something else?"

"Like what?" Veronica demanded.

"I don't know! But we have to find her!"

"Don't you think she's probably who the cops are after?" Trixie held her palms up. "They wouldn't have run out of here the way they did if they weren't certain they knew who the killer was. Frank was probably calling to tell them the lab found cyanide in the food, and it was either Cheryl or Donna."

"It was Donna! We have to go make sure they're getting the right woman! What if they're wasting time going after Cheryl?"

"Maybe it is Cheryl."

"It's *not* Cheryl! How many times do I have to tell you? Now, who's coming with me?"

"Why don't you call the police station and tell them, if you're so sure?" Trixie asked.

"You think they're going to listen to me instead of Mitchell and Darren? They won't even pass on a message to them."

Thunder crashed again, and the lights flickered.

Aunt Star put her hands on her hips. "If you don't call, I will."

"Fine. I'll call."

I opened the pantry door, and we trooped out. I grabbed the phone off the wall and put it to my ear, but there was no dial tone. I flipped the hook a few times, but it remained silent.

"Phone's dead." I put the phone back and turned to the others. "I'm going. Who's with me?"

Aunt Star stepped forward. "I'm in."

Trixie raised her hand. "I'll drive, but I'm not confronting anyone."

Veronica seemed torn, for once. "You know I want to go, but with the visitation starting soon ..."

I got right up in her face. "Would you rather make small talk or catch another killer?"

"Well, when you put it that way ..."

"Come on, then. There's no more time to waste."

I grabbed my purse, opened the door to the hall, and bumped into Greg again.

"Sorry."

We took off down the hall, with Greg calling after us, "Where are you going?"

"We'll fill you in later! Keep things running here."

Trixie, with her long legs, was in the lead, but she came to a halt at the door. "It's raining buckets out there."

I peered out. "Look how dark it is. We'll take my car. It's the closest."

I tossed Trixie the keys, and she held the door open for the rest of us. We dashed through the torrential rain to my car. Veronica tried the passenger door. "It's locked! Why in the world is it locked?"

"There's a killer on the loose."

Trixie got the driver's door unlocked and pushed the seatback forward so I could scramble into the backseat. I reached through to unlock the other door. A rain-soaked Aunt Star joined me in the back, and Veronica dropped into the passenger seat. Meanwhile, Trixie fired up the engine, so as soon as Veronica slammed her door, we were off.

"Where to?" Trixie threw over her shoulder at me.

"Donna's! Go! Go!"

"I'm going. Cool your jets."

In her haste, Trixie nearly skidded us through the stoplight.

Thankfully nobody was coming, so she continued through town. She slowed as we approached Donna's house. No lights were on, Donna's car wasn't in the carport, and no police cars were in sight. We came to a halt at the curb in front of the house.

"Nobody's home," Trixie stated. "Now what?"

If there was anybody Donna was as upset with as she was with Paula, it would likely be Jeff.

"Jeff's!" I yelled. "Step on it!"

We took off again, and Veronica turned in her seat to look at me. I almost laughed at the sight of her wet hair plastered against her head.

She asked, "Are you going to tell us why you think it's Donna?"

"I don't *think* it's Donna. I know it's Donna."

"Well?"

As we sped through the streets of Cherry Hill, I filled them in on my conversation with Billy—at least part of it. They didn't need to know everything he'd said.

Lightning flashed across the sky, and a few seconds later, all the streetlights and the lights in the houses around us went dead. "Power's out," I said unnecessarily.

Trixie screeched to a halt in front of Jeff's house. With the power out, it was difficult to tell if anyone was home.

"Pull into the drive," I said.

"Really?"

"Yes, really. His garage is around back. Do *you* want to walk around there in the rain to see if his pickup's in it?"

She put the car back in gear and turned into the driveway. We pulled past the house to see the overhead door to the large, detached garage was up, and water was flooding in. Jeff's truck wasn't there, nor was Donna's car.

"Should we close the garage for him?" Trixie asked.

"No!"

"Where to next? Where else could she be?"

I closed my eyes and wracked my brain. I turned to Aunt Star. "Didn't you say you saw Randy's truck outside Donna's house the other day?"

She nodded.

"Okay then. Off to the Stouffer farm!"

Trixie reversed out of the driveway, and we headed out of town. A few minutes later we turned down the lane to the farm. The power was on out there, as a pole light was on, but no lights shone from the farmhouse windows, and no vehicles were parked in the drive. When we pulled up to the house, I noticed a light in the barn further down the lane.

"Go back to the barn," I ordered.

We continued down the lane and around the barn, where the large barn door was open. Randy's truck was pulled inside, and he was leaned against it, smoking a cigarette. His face held a puzzled look, but he raised a hand in greeting and then motioned for us to pull into the open spot beside his truck.

"Get out! Get out!"

Trixie nimbly jumped out of the car and then pulled me out of the backseat.

"What's going on here, ladies?" He leaned down to see who else was in the car.

"Is Donna here?" I put my hands on my hips.

"No." He took a drag of his cigarette. Randy had never been one to get in a hurry about much of anything that wasn't happening on a football field. "Why would she be?"

"I don't know, really." I let my arms drop.

I turned my head when the cigarette smoke drifted in front of my face, and I focused on Randy's truck. Where had I seen it recently? I closed my eyes, and I recalled it was the truck I thought I saw twice when Aunt Star and I left The Blue Barn Saturday night. My eyes popped open.

"Does somebody else have a truck exactly like this?" I asked Randy.

He turned his head to blow smoke over his shoulder. "Yep. Marty James bought one last week."

Everything clicked. That hadn't been Randy's truck outside Donna's house. It was Marty's! I must have been right that something was going on between the two of them.

"Back in the car!" I dove into the backseat and pulled the driver's seat back. "Get in, Trix!"

Randy leaned down to look at me. "Where you off to?"

"You'll probably hear about it later."

"Be careful, whatever you're doing," he said before slamming Trixie's door shut.

Trixie backed out of the barn. "Where *are* we off to?"

"Marty's."

"Marty's?" Aunt Star echoed.

"He and Donna must be a couple. Remember I asked about that the other day? That wasn't Randy's truck you saw at Donna's. It was Marty's."

"But why would Donna be at Marty's now?"

"I don't know, but it's as good a place to look as any, isn't it?"

Marty's house was outside the other side of town, so we headed back through Cherry Hill. The rain was letting up, but the power was still out.

When we left the city limits, we could see the top of Marty's house over the half-grown corn in the field that surrounded the house. Kyle's Jeep was turning into the driveway ahead of us. Trixie slowed down, and once we got past the field, we watched Kyle enter the house. I then registered that Jeff's truck was in the drive but Marty's wasn't. We pulled in beside the Jeep.

"Look! Donna's car is in the shed." I pointed.

"Yes, but what are *we* going to do?" Trixie shifted the car into park. "Surely those two men can handle her."

"I'm going in," I declared. "I don't know what's happening in there, or if the men are in danger. Who's coming?"

I pushed Trixie's seat forward, and she pressed back against it. "Not me. Scott would never forgive me. I gotta think of the kids."

"You're right," I said. "You stay here as the getaway driver. Aunt Star?"

"Darren would kill me. And you told me yourself not to mess up what I have with him."

"Thanks for throwing my words back in my face. But I get it." I leaned into the space between the front seats. "Well, Veronica," I felt bold enough to use her first name, "you coming with me or not?"

"I can't let you go in alone, so I guess I am."

She stepped out into the misting rain, and I scrambled over Aunt Star to join her.

TWENTY-ONE

"LET'S GO AROUND TO the back of the house," I said. "See if we can peek in the back door or a window or something."

As soon as we stepped off the gravel drive, my heels sank into the soaked ground. I kicked the shoes off and continued without them. Veronica did the same.

Mud squished through my pantyhose and between my toes as we crept around the side of the house and over to the steps leading to the back door. The windows were too high for us to see in, but the back door contained a large window.

I crept up the steps and peeked in. The door led into the kitchen, and Donna was facing my direction. My eyes widened when I spotted the shotgun in her hands. I dropped back down out of sight, but I knew she had seen me.

"Go!" I whispered to Veronica. "She has a gun, and she saw me. Get around the side of the house. Now."

Veronica scuttled away. I could have followed her and tried to get away too, but I didn't want to lead Donna to my friends. She didn't need to know anyone else was with me.

The door swung open, and Donna ordered, "Get in here, Becky." Her gun wasn't trained on me, but I wasn't about to argue, so I stepped inside with my hands up as the rain started coming down in earnest again.

Jeff was duct taped to a kitchen chair in the darkened room, tape covered his mouth, and his eyes were droopy but open. Two plastic cups sat on the table. Kyle stood in the middle of the room with his hands up.

"Get over there by Kyle." Donna motioned with the gun.

My hose-clad feet were covered in mud, and I slipped and fell after a few steps. Kyle made a move toward me, but Donna stuck the gun barrel in his chest. "Don't move."

"Get up." She jerked her head at me.

I scrambled to my feet and stood near Kyle, water dripping from my hair and the hem of my dress. Donna grabbed a roll of duct tape from the table and handed it to me. "Tape his hands together behind his back."

I stepped behind Kyle, who put his hands behind him. He pressed one hand against a black, rectangular object in his back pocket, but I couldn't tell what it was and didn't really care. I picked at the edge of the tape, but it was stuck.

"Hurry up!" Donna said.

"It's real sticky. I can't get it started."

She huffed out a breath.

"Why are you doing this?" I shot a quick glance around Kyle. "And why did you kill Paula?"

"You figured it out, huh? Even before this?"

"Yes."

"That witch is the reason my marriage broke up. She was little miss perfect, wasn't she?" Donna waved the gun toward Jeff, and he struggled against the tape. "At least *he* thought so. 'Why can't you be more like Paula?' 'See how Paula keeps their house so nice?'" she mimicked. "Ugh! And watching him act all charming around her made me want to vomit. Then once we knew I couldn't give him babies, that was it. He was done."

Jeff moaned loudly, and I took a quick glance at him. His eyes were full of sadness.

"I'm so sorry about that, Donna." I finally got the tape started and it pulled away from the roll with a screech. "That must have been really hard."

"Get the tape on him," she ordered. "And then get back out here where I can see you."

"Can I say something?" Kyle asked.

"No!" Donna and I both yelled.

Donna continued, "Then Paula got pregnant, which was hard for me, but I tried my best to be happy for her. Then after the baby was born, her whole personality changed. I called her one time, and she went on and on about her perfect marriage and her perfect child, and she laughed at me because I'd never have that. What kind of person does that? Huh?" She waved her gun at me. "Tape him up, already. Stop standing there staring at me."

Kyle put his hands back-to-back, and I rolled the tape lightly around his wrists, making sure to give him some wiggle room. After wrapping it around a few times, I tried to tear off the end, but it wouldn't budge.

"What's the problem back there?" Donna asked.

"I can't tear the tape. Are there some scissors or something?"

"Do I look dumb? I'm not giving you a weapon."

"Well, I don't know what you want me to do."

"Use your teeth."

I bit the edge of the tape with my teeth, and I wondered what my friends were up to outside. I prayed they'd come up with a plan to rescue us, and soon. The tape began to tear, and I pulled it the rest of the way off. I didn't put the tape roll down, but Donna didn't notice.

"What are you going to do now?" I moved out from behind Kyle. "And why is Jeff all taped up, anyway?"

"Because he needs to pay for what he did to me."

"Like Paula paid?" I nodded my head toward Jeff. "Did you poison him too?" That could explain how she managed to tape him up and why he wasn't fully lucid.

She trained the gun at me. "Yes. Not enough to kill him, though. I wanted to make him suffer a while before ending it."

"Why are you even here? And why is Jeff here?"

"I called and told him Marty had punched and kicked me, and he came running. I think I did a good job of pretending to be hurt. Didn't I, Jeff?"

I took another look at Jeff, whose eyes were glistening with unshed tears. It was difficult to believe anyone would think Marty would lay a hand on a woman, but it wasn't difficult to believe Jeff would come to a battered woman's aid, no matter who she was.

"You and Marty are dating?" I asked, to keep her talking instead of thinking about shooting us.

"We've gone out a few times. Wouldn't really call it dating." She shrugged.

I couldn't believe how calm she was or that she seemed to be in no hurry to finish what she had started. Then again, she had killed someone and gone about her life as if nothing out of the ordinary had happened, so I shouldn't have been surprised.

She swung the gun toward Jeff. "I figured if he was found out here, nobody would suspect me."

I shook my head at the fact that she was perfectly fine with setting Marty and Kyle up for Jeff's murder.

"Are you planning to shoot all of us or what?" Kyle asked her.

I clamped my mouth shut so I wouldn't yell at him again.

Donna swung the gun back toward us, and I took a closer look at it. I didn't know a lot about guns, but I was fairly certain a double-barreled shotgun only held two shells. At least, that made sense in my brain. I moved a little further away from Kyle.

"You can't shoot all of us, can you?" I asked. "You don't have enough shells."

"That's what I was trying to tell you earlier!" Kyle said.

"Shut up, Kyle!" Donna growled at him.

"You should have spit it out, man," I said. "You don't need

my permission to save my life."

"I don't know why I didn't have you put tape over his mouth," Donna said.

"Sorry," Kyle muttered in my direction.

Donna continued, "And I don't know why the two of you had to show up and screw this all up for me."

"I do live here," Kyle said under his breath.

I took another step away from him. "You can't get away with this, Donna. Even if you kill two of us, there will still be one of us left to tell the tale."

"Not if I kill you and Kyle first and then reload. He can't stop me." She used the gun to point at Jeff, who whimpered.

I decided to take a chance, considering we outnumbered her. "Yeah, but my friends can. They're right outside. In fact, they should have had time to go get the police by now."

"You're lying."

"I'm not."

As if on cue, a soaking-wet Mitchell appeared behind Donna in the open doorway into the living room and held a finger over his lips. Kyle or Jeff must have reacted to seeing him, because Donna looked over her shoulder. Over the course of the next few seconds, I threw the tape at Donna and dropped to the floor, Mitchell knocked the gun barrel upward, Donna pulled the trigger, Kyle hit the floor next to me, Mitchell wrestled the gun out of Donna's hands, and Darren entered and leveled his handgun at Donna's head.

"Anybody hit?" Darren yelled.

I got to my knees and leaned over Kyle, who was curled up in the fetal position with his hands still taped behind his back. I gasped when I spotted blood on his shirt. "Kyle's hurt!"

"I'll be fine," he said through clenched teeth. "She hit my shoulder. Hopefully only a few pellets."

When I looked up, Mitchell was snapping handcuffs on

Donna, and Frank trained his gun on her side. Mitchell appeared calm as he read Donna her rights, but his eyes betrayed his anger. They softened slightly when we briefly locked gazes, but not enough for my liking. He nudged Donna into the front room.

"She poisoned Jeff," I said, "but she claimed it wasn't enough to kill him. Didn't say what type of poison, though."

Darren spoke into his walkie talkie and then kneeled next to Kyle. "Two ambulances will be here soon." Cherry County only had two ambulances, so I was glad nobody else was injured.

"Can somebody get the tape off me?" Kyle groaned. "And off Jeff? We keep scissors in the end drawer."

By the time I dug the scissors out, sirens sounded outside, and multiple officers entered the house. Frank took the scissors from me and released the two men from their bonds. I sank into a kitchen chair, my adrenaline gone, and dropped my head into my hands. Seconds later, a strong hand gripped my shoulder. I looked up into Mitchell's face, but he wouldn't meet my eyes.

"Why don't you come with me?" He took me by the elbow and ushered me into the front room. "Let's talk outside." His tone was clipped.

"But it's raining."

"It just stopped. The sky is clearing."

He led me outside but stopped at the sight of all the vehicles and officers in the driveway. "Let's go around there." He turned me toward the far end of the house, where we could talk around the corner without being seen. "You okay to walk out here without shoes?"

"I did it earlier. I'll be fine."

I stepped off the sidewalk and my foot slipped right out from under me. He caught me before I could hit the ground and swept me up into his arms. I wrapped my arms around his neck, but he still wouldn't look at me, though our faces were inches apart. We rounded the corner and he carefully set me on my feet. Then he stepped back, turned away from me, and looked out over the cornfield. He was no longer wearing his suit coat, and his white dress shirt was plastered to his back.

He reached down and picked up a rock at his feet. "Do you know how it feels when you're told someone you care about is being held at gunpoint by a known killer?" He threw the rock as hard and as far as he could into the field. The cornstalks rustled when it fell.

"No," I said in a small voice.

He flung another rock and then shoved his hands into his pockets. "Do you know how it feels when that happens even after you told the person not to get involved—for their own safety—but they did it anyway?" He finally turned and looked at me.

"Pretty sure I'd be mad."

"You think?" he retorted.

"But I'd also be glad, if it turned out they were okay," I said hopefully.

His stony facade cracked a little. "I am extremely glad you're okay. But that's not the point."

"Part of the point?" I took a step toward him, and he didn't retreat.

"Still not *the* point ... but maybe *a* point," he conceded.

I closed the gap between us and slipped my arms around his waist. He didn't move, but he looked down into my eyes.

"Don't you ever do that again." He sighed. "I won't survive it."

"I'm confident you would, but I'll try not to do it again."

"Try?"

"That's the best I can promise. You don't want me to lie to you, do you?"

He sighed again, took his hands out of his pockets, tucked my head under his chin, and wrapped his arms around my shoulders.

We stood like that for at least a minute while I felt his heartrate slowly decrease. Then he whispered, "No, I don't want you to ever lie to me."

I leaned my head back. "Are you going to kiss me now or what? Even if I am a witness?"

"You really need to stop being a witness to these ridiculous crimes." He gave me a slight smile.

"I'll do my best. At least I'm not a suspect for this one."

I stood on my tiptoes, but without my shoes on, I couldn't quite reach his mouth. When I stepped up onto his shoes, he chuckled.

"You're getting my nice shoes all muddy."

"They were muddy already. Now shut up and kiss me."

He finally bent his head down toward me. Minutes could have passed before a cough caught our attention. I pulled slightly away from Mitchell and stepped off his shoes, but he didn't let me go, so I peeked back over my shoulder.

Darren said to me, "When you're done here, your aunt would like to see you. She's in my car." He spun on his heel and left us alone again.

Mitchell pulled me in tightly again and kissed the top of my head. "You've got your orders," he said into my hair.

I rested a hand over his heart. "I really am sorry I scared you."

"I know you are. But try your best not to do it again."

"And thanks for rescuing me."

"Seems to be becoming a habit. It's one I'd like to break."

I leaned back and looked up at him. "You don't like rescuing me?"

"Rescuing you is rather satisfying. But I don't like it when you need to be rescued." He slid his hands down my back. "What I *do* like is this dress. It's a little distracting, though, especially as it's drenched, and you weren't supposed to distract me tonight."

He broke out into a smile. "Oh, here it comes. Hello, Mr. Blush."

"Detective Crowe?"

I didn't recognize the voice, so I stepped away from Mitchell as a young, uniformed officer came around the corner.

"There you are," he said, his eyes darting back and forth between us. "We need you inside."

"I'll be there in a minute," Mitchell said. "I have one more question for Miss Monahan."

The officer nodded and headed back around the house.

I cocked my head at Mitchell. "What's your question, Detective Crowe?"

"That was a delay tactic, but I do have a personal question." He pulled me to him once more. "When this case is wrapped up, would you like to go on a date with me? A real date?"

A smile spread across my face. "One where nobody gets murdered, you don't have to rescue me, and we don't have to sneak around corners to make out?"

He nodded and then grinned. "Though sneaking around is rather fun."

TWENTY-TWO

BY THE TIME AN officer dropped Aunt Star and me off at home, the power was back on, but we immediately discovered a different problem. The house was locked, and we didn't have a key.

The police had sent Trixie and Veronica home soon after they arrived on the scene, and the two took my car, with my purse still inside. Aunt Star's purse and keys were still in the church pantry.

We stopped the officer before he pulled out of the drive, and he took us to Trixie's house. My car sat in the driveway next to Scott's pickup.

Scott answered the door and handed me my purse.

"Thanks. Can we talk to Trixie for a minute?"

"She's in the shower," he said in a terse voice. He didn't invite us in. "I can't believe you dragged her into this." He crossed his arms and stared daggers at me.

I put my hands on my hips. "I didn't drag her into anything, Scott Wallace. She made her own choice to come along. Plus, she may have saved my life."

I had discovered that when Veronica told Trixie and Aunt Star what was happening in the house, Trixie immediately left for the police station. Veronica and my aunt stayed behind, huddled down in the front seat of Kyle's Jeep. He had left the keys in it, so they knew they could get away if needed.

"She wouldn't have needed to save your life if you had stayed at the church," he said.

"Yeah, but we probably saved Jeff and Kyle's lives by going out there."

He shook his head in frustration but said, "I'll give you that. But I'm still mad at you."

"That's fair. I get it."

He was in good company. Darren was ticked at me too, for obvious reasons.

"Thanks, Scott," Aunt Star said. "We'll see you later." She pulled me off the porch and toward the car.

On the way home, I said, "It's only 6:30. Are we going to the visitation?"

"Do you think it's still on?" she asked. "After all this?"

"I wonder if anyone has even told Billy and his family yet."

"Surely somebody did."

"Well, we can't not go, if it's still happening. Right?" I was exhausted in every way possible, but I wanted to be there for Billy and Georgia. Still, a part of me hoped Aunt Star would order me to stay home.

She sighed. "All I want to do is take a warm bath and then crawl into bed. But we do need to go. You'll regret it if you don't, and I won't let you go alone."

I grabbed her hand. "Thanks."

A tear slid down my cheek, and she squeezed my hand.

"That's what aunts are for."

———

AN HOUR LATER, we pulled back out of the drive in fresh black dresses and shoes. We sat on trash bags, since the seats were still damp from earlier. The phones were still down, so we didn't know if the visitation was still happening, but even if it wasn't, we wanted to find out the latest news, and we couldn't do that from home. Darren had told us to come to the station in the morning to give our statements, but we'd go tonight if that meant we could find out what was going on.

The church parking lot was full, which answered our question about the visitation. We found a parking spot down the street and made our way to the front doors. An older couple I recognized but didn't know well exited as we climbed the steps. They studied us with interest but only nodded a greeting.

The funeral director stood inside the doors. He held out his hand for me to shake. I grasped it, and he covered my hand with his left for a second. Then he did the same to Aunt Star.

"Ladies," Mr. Cooper said, "Officer Nichols stopped by a few minutes before we opened the doors. I'm so glad they—" he looked me in the eye"—*you* put an end to this madness. It's hard to believe it was Donna Jenkins, though."

"Yes," I replied. "I never would have thought her capable of it."

He swept his hand toward the open double doors into the sanctuary. "Go on in there. I know the family will all be glad to see you."

Though the room was nearly full of people, the receiving line was short. Most of the mourners had already greeted the family and were sitting in the pews or standing in the back. The chatter quieted and more than a few heads turned to watch us as we made our way to the end of the line.

We reached Billy, and he pulled me into a tight embrace. "Thank you," he whispered. When he pulled back, tears streamed down both of our faces. I itched to wipe his tears away, as it was disconcerting to see him cry, but that wasn't my place. His mother pressed tissues into our hands.

He wiped his eyes, leaned down to my ear, and whispered, "I shouldn't have said what I did earlier. It wasn't fair to Paula."

"Forget it," I murmured back. "I already have."

He straightened again and gave my hands a squeeze. "I can't

believe you put yourself in that kind of danger. I'm grateful, and I'm sure Jeff and Kyle's families are as well. But please don't do something like that ever again."

If I were a man, nobody would be trying to talk me out of rescuing anyone, but I wasn't about to call him out on it. I diplomatically said, "I'll keep your advice in mind," and smiled at him.

After we spoke with Georgia and the rest of Paula's family, I pulled Aunt Star out the side door of the sanctuary so we wouldn't have to talk to anyone else. I didn't have the energy for it.

———

THE PHONE WAS WORKING by the time we returned home, so I called Mom to tell her about the evening's events. Unsurprisingly, I got an earful from both her and Dad about the danger I put myself in. But before we hung up, they both told me they were proud of me.

I was fast asleep in bed when the ringing phone woke me up. After two rings, it stopped. Shortly after, Aunt Star yelled down the hall, "Are you awake? It's for you!"

I stretched, rolled over, and fumbled around in the dark until I found the phone on my nightstand. "Hello?" I said drowsily as I lay my head back on my pillow.

The line clicked, indicating Aunt Star had hung up her extension.

"Hey there."

I smiled at the sound of Mitchell's voice. "Hey."

"Did I wake you up?"

"Yes, but I don't care."

He chuckled. "You okay?"

"We'll get to me in a minute. Tell me about Kyle and Jeff.

Are they going to be all right?"

"Yes, Kyle's wounds were mostly superficial. He got the outer edge of the blast. And Jeff will be fine in a few days."

"Did Jeff say anything about what happened?"

"He wasn't coherent when they took him away, but Darren spoke with him a little while ago. He was understandably angry with Donna but also with himself for believing Marty would hurt a woman. He said if he hadn't gone out there, he might not have put Kyle and you in danger."

"Leave it to Jeff to think this was all his fault," I said.

"He also swore he didn't divorce Donna because she couldn't have kids. He wanted both you and Kyle to know that. At that point their marriage was already beyond repair."

"I'm glad to hear that. Not that their marriage was beyond repair, but that he didn't divorce her for that reason. Jeff has his issues, but once I had time to think about everything Donna had said, it was difficult for me to believe that was true."

"Now back to you," Mitchell said. "How are you dealing with what happened tonight?"

"I don't know, really. I'm so tired right now it's hard to think straight."

"I won't keep you long, but I stopped by The Osh to change into some dry clothes and wanted to check on you. We'll see you in the morning, right?"

"Yes, I'll stop by before work to give my statement." I rolled over onto my back and stared into the darkness.

"I'm sure they'd give you the day off, considering the circumstances."

"They would, but we have Paula's funeral, so I'd be going there anyway."

"I'm so focused on the case I'd forgotten about the funeral."

"Hey, where did you and Darren go when you left the church this evening?"

I reached over and turned on the lamp on my nightstand, adjusted my pillows, and sat up against them while Mitchell talked. I was afraid I'd fall asleep if I didn't.

"We got a call that there was a trace of cyanide in Donna's applesauce—not enough to kill anyone, but enough to make people sick. We rushed over to her house, but she wasn't there or at Jeff's, so we went back to the station to regroup and try to figure out where she might be. That's where we were when Trixie came barreling into the parking lot to find us. How did you know where to go?"

"Well, it took me four tries before I got the right place." I told him where we went and why. "I guess we were right behind you guys at Donna's and Jeff's. I'm surprised we didn't pass you on the road somewhere."

"You have some solid investigative skills," Mitchell said. "Cherry Hill PD should hire you."

I laughed. "I think Darren would have a different opinion on that."

"Probably so."

"Plus, since I'm not a police officer, I don't have to follow protocol."

He chuckled. "That is helpful."

"And I like my job."

"You're good at it."

I smiled. "How do you know?"

"Because you always want to help people. It's who you are."

I blushed, but for a different reason than usual.

"Thanks," I said sincerely.

"You're most welcome."

I shifted the phone to my other ear. "How long is this case going to take? I can't imagine it'll move as quickly as the last one, especially after what happened tonight."

"Interestingly, we have a recording of what happened at Kyle and Marty's house."

"Are you kidding me? How? There wasn't even electricity!"

"Kyle had one of those mini-cassette recorders in his back pocket. He said he uses it at work. He was able to hit the record button without Donna noticing."

"No way! He tried to alert me to something in his pocket, but I couldn't tell what it was. Good old Kyle. I bet that makes your job a lot easier."

"Most definitely. That should also make the whole process move along much faster."

"Good."

"Better than good."

We were both silent for a moment.

"I'd better get down to the station," he said reluctantly. "Still lots to do tonight."

"I'll see you in the morning."

"Sweet dreams."

If he was in them, they'd be sweet indeed.

Have you read Book 1 in the Totally 80s Mysteries series?

Coming
Fall 2022

Of
HEIST
and
MEN

Totally
80s
Mysteries
Book 3

Mystery Journals

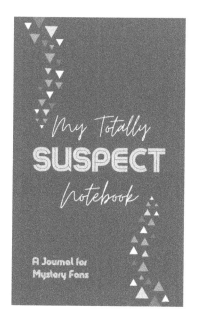 

Do you want an easy way to keep track of all the suspects or other characters in mysteries? These journals allow mystery readers to record suspects, other characters, motives, means, opportunity, and more!

Available at Amazon.com

About the Author

D.A. (Dana) Wilkerson is the author of the Totally 80s Mysteries cozy mystery series. She has been a professional writer and editor for almost two decades and was the collaborative writer of two non-fiction *New York Times* best sellers: *The Vow: The True Events That Inspired the Movie* (Kim and Krickitt Carpenter) and *Balancing It All* (Candace Cameron Bure).

Dana lives in Oklahoma and enjoys traveling, reading, being an aunt, binge-watching crime shows, and attending Oklahoma City Thunder basketball games.

FOLLOW

D.A. Wilkerson
on social media!

Instagram
@d.a.wilkerson.author

Facebook
@dawilkersonauthor

Tiktok
@dawilkersonauthor

CPSIA information can be obtained
at www.ICGtesting.com
Printed in the USA
LVHW101701161022
730832LV00018B/440